AF192129

JAMES AURELIEN

Bluebell

novum ⬤ pro

www.novumpublishing.nl

© 2022 novum publishing

ISBN 978-3-99131-075-4
Geredigeerd door: Angelo Gardener
Omslagfotos: Wabeno, Kdshutterman, Ivan Sizov, Akinshin, SERGEYSHKODA, Elisanth | Dreamstime.com
Ontwerp omslag, lay-out & typografie: novum publishing
Foto binnendeel:
Burlesck | Dreamstime.com

www.novumpublishing.nl

Climate neutral
Print product
ClimatePartner.com/16547-2201-1002

Content warning

This book contains content
that some readers may find upsetting.
If this is of concern to you, please see the extensive
content warning list at the end of the book.

Contents

Chapter One
A Close Call 9

Chapter Two
Fey 12

Chapter Three
Down the Rabbit Hole 18

Chapter Four
Redrum 24

Chapter Five
Rock Bottom 31

Chapter Six
Devlin 36

Chapter Seven
The Cemetery 46

Chapter Eight
Rosabella 50

Chapter Nine
Rune 63

Chapter Ten
Vices 66

Chapter Eleven
Ubel 72

Chapter Twelve
Gotcha 78

Chapter Thirteen
Home Sweet Home 92

Chapter Fourteen
Endora 103

Chapter Fifteen
Peripeteia 112

Chapter Sixteen
Carnage 117

Chapter Seventeen
Trespassing 125

Chapter Eighteen
Lycanthropy 132

Chapter Nineteen
Larua 136

Chapter Twenty
Oliver 149

Chapter Twenty-One
Winds of Change 162

Chapter Twenty-Two
One Hundred and Seventy-One 171

Chapter Twenty-Three
Full Circle 186

Chapter One
A Close Call

"Junie? Junie! Oh, you're awake!"

I looked up into my mother's teary eyes realizing I felt dizzy, nauseous and just not right.

"Mum," I mumbled.

"Yes, dear! Oh, I'm so glad you're all right!"

A tear rolled down from behind her glasses and fell to the floor. My father stood behind her with his hand on her shoulder. He was smiling, looking relieved and was also teary eyed. On the other side of my bed I saw my friend Callista, who had tears rolling down both her cheeks, smudging her make-up.

"What happened?" It was hard to form the words. It was even harder to focus on anything. I couldn't remember why I was in this white, bright room which I could only assume was a hospital room. It smelt like a hospital too.

"You got hurt, dear," my mother explained. She stepped forward and ran her hands through my curls affectionately. "You were at the wrong place at the wrong time. You were walking home from work and … a car hit you."

I squinted and tried to remember the event, but the last thing I could remember was walking out of the coffee house I worked at; Better Beans. Everything else was a blur.

"Why did it hit me?" My words sounded more like moaning than talking, as it hurt to speak.

"You did nothing wrong, child. The driver was drunk and crashed right onto the sidewalk where you were walking. He hit you and then crashed into a building," my father said, speaking in a mix of sadness and anger.

"Did anyone else get hurt?"

My mother smiled, she seemed moved, and stepped back to stand at the foot-end of the bed. "You're the one in a hospital bed and you still manage to ask that question …"

My father didn't go off the topic. "Only the driver. He died on the spot."

I looked around the room. Everything hurt. The lights were too bright. The bed felt too hard even though it was probably perfectly fine. My whole body was aching.

"Do you remember anything?" asked Callista. She reached out to grab my hand.

"Not really … I was just walking home," I said as I squeezed her hand softly. As I was speaking some things popped back into my head. "I remember the headlights."

I closed my eyes, and a vivid scenario came back to me; I was just walking when I heard tires screeching behind me and when I'd turned around, I looked directly into the bright headlights of a car coming right at me at full speed.

When I opened my eyes again, I saw Callista nodding. I looked at my parents, they both had a worried look on their faces.

"I don't remember the crash," I said as I closed my eyes again, trying to remember. "I do remember waking up."

At the site of the crash, I had woken up after being hit, and there was a woman with me. She had piercing blue eyes and had looked mortified when our eyes locked. Thinking about it gave me a weird feeling but at the time it was the least of my concerns, so I brushed it off.

"There was a girl. A woman. I think she woke me up … but I passed out again. When I woke up again, they were checking on me … the ambulance people. The police were there too. There was a crowd. It smelt like smoke. It was loud. I got carried into an ambulance … and then I woke up here."

I opened my eyes again to see that both of my parents' eyes were watery again. Callista was still holding my hand, tears still rolling.

"It's okay," I mumbled in an attempt to soothe them. "I'm okay." It was dead silent for a minute. "Am I okay?"

Callista chuckled. "You broke your hip, five ribs and your arm. You have bruises and stitches, but luckily none of it will be permanent," my mother answered.

I nodded, at least as much as I could.

"Why don't you get some rest, dear? The doctor said she wants you here for a few more days just to be sure you're okay. We'll be back later."

"Thank you," I squeezed it out.

"We love you, baby," my father added. They gave me a loving smile and walked out. Callista squeezed my hand this time.

"See you later, sweetie," she said, then walked out too.

I fell right back into a blissful, sedated sleep.

Chapter Two

Fey

Over the next few months my body started to heal. I hadn't been able to work in a while, so my parents had been supporting me and helped me around the house while I tried to put myself back together. My friends were also helping, bringing me food, running errands, whatever they could do. Much to my displeasure – I felt like a burden, but resting was starting to pay off; slowly but surely, my body started to recover. My mind, however, was a different story; I was scared. Despite the therapy appointments I had been taking, I was scared to leave the house, scared of cars, scared of loud noises. Life had become scary. On top of that there was one thing I hadn't talked to anyone about; I had been having very vivid nightmares.

At first, I thought they didn't scare me *that* much – they were just dreams, after all – but I'd still wake up shaking and drenched in sweat. Then the nightmares progressively got worse until I became too scared to sleep and I couldn't lie to myself anymore about not being scared. The nightmares were always different, but they ended the same; I died.

It was always a painful and terrifying death. Electrocution, drowning, getting stabbed, getting shot … Besides the fact that I always died they had one more thing in common; whether I'd be murdered or die in some other way, the blue-eyed, red-haired woman I saw on the day of the accident was always there. She could have been the murderer or she would watch me die and do nothing. Sometimes she would smile. I had no idea who she was, and it didn't seem like she had done anything to me when I saw her that day, but within a matter of months this stranger had become my worst fear.

I kept telling myself that these dreams were just a manifestation of anxiety, that I didn't know this woman and that she hadn't hurt me, and that she wouldn't in the future. I had no factual reason to believe otherwise.

Another night I woke up drenched in sweat. I was shaking and out of breath. With great effort I took a sip from the glass of water on my nightstand and sighed. My alarm would go off in a few hours; it was the first day I'd go back to work at the coffeehouse. I was looking forward to it but I wasn't looking forward to the lack of sleep I'd have to deal with. Coming to terms with the fact that I wouldn't be able to sleep anymore, I decided to turn on my television and channel-hop. Before I got to a channel I wanted to watch, I came across the news. There was a fragment that caught my attention, about a teenage boy who had gone missing the day before. The boy was living in a hospice and had gone out for a walk but never returned. His caretakers said he went on the same walk every single day and there was no reason for him not to come back. It was unlike him. Everyone was really worried about him. I hoped they would find the poor boy.

When I arrived at work later, my boss didn't put me straight back into waitressing but gave me tasks that I could do without overworking my body, considering I had broken several bones in the accident. Most of them had healed or at least started to heal but my body was still tender.

I spent the day taking and making phone calls, answering e-mails, ordering supplies, and occasionally processing a few orders at the counter, so I had the chance to stand up and walk around a little.

I was enjoying a decaf soy latte on my lunch break when a gorgeous little butterfly found its way inside the office space in the back and settled on the wall across from me. It stayed there until my shift was over.

Funnily enough, when I opened the door hours later to go home, the butterfly flew out the door.

After my walk home, I was relieved to have made my way back safely and concluded that it had been a good day. On the evening news I saw the missing boy again, there were still no leads.

At around sunset a cat I had never seen before found its way inside my house through an open window, walked around for a bit and then before I could put it outside made its own way out again. It was curious but I didn't think much of it. *It wouldn't be the first time a strange cat had ever infiltrated someone's house*, I thought.

For the next few days, and evenings, the days remained enjoyable, but the nights continued to be harrowing. The same graphic, terrifyingly realistic nightmares every single night had started to take a toll on my body … I was feeling exhausted every single day and had developed a new fear of death. It manifested in the fear of eating: what if someone poisoned me? What if my food was contaminated? And fear of people: what if they're out to get me? What if they are armed? You name it …

I had just begun recovering from the expected fears caused by a potentially fatal car accident, but it was starting to feel as if it had all been for nothing. Undeniably, fear was now ruling my life. It felt as if I was living in one of the thriller shows I always loved to watch, or maybe one of the true crime shows. Who knew? All I knew was that I didn't like it one bit, and the shows weren't so great anymore either.

On a rainy Friday morning at the end of the week I had called in sick, because I was so fatigued and anxiety ridden that it was simply too much for me to leave the house.

Since my night had been filled with terror once more, I was up early and caught the morning news while the sun was rising.

Another person had gone missing.

It was the second person reported missing within a month, something that had never happened before in the small town of Cunabula.

The sick boy had still not been found and now there was another missing person's case. This time an elderly woman had gone missing. She was taking a stroll in a park in the early morning and never returned. Her caregiver went inside to look when the old lady didn't answer the door for their morning visit, and found no one inside and called the police. Later, they found her walker still in the park but there was no trace of the woman. The police were expecting the worst.

I turned the television off and sighed. News like this didn't make me feel any better when I was already terrified of the world.

I tried to shrug it off and told myself it must have been an accident, just like with the missing boy. These were accidents. Soon they would be found, and they would either be well and had just been lost, or some unfortunate accident had happened; there was no foul play, I concluded. There couldn't have been. With that in mind, I decided to go and have the breakfast that my extremely understanding boss had offered me.

He had empathy for the situation I was in and told me it would be good for me to get some fresh air, go outside and interact with someone.

So, I went outside, looking exactly how I felt (not good) and started to mooch towards the coffeehouse. It being early July, the weather was pleasantly warm with a light breeze dancing through the trees. The streets were filled with people rushing to get to work.

It was only a ten-minute walk to work from my home but considering I was walking extremely slowly, it might have taken me a bit longer on that particular day.

I was looking at some flowers on the sidewalk when I was startled by a dog barking on the sidewalk across the road to my left. Much to my horror, my eyes fell on the woman who I had seen on the day of the accident and since then in my nightmares, every single night.

I froze in the middle of the street and felt my chest tighten. I couldn't breathe. My legs suddenly felt heavy. I felt dizzy. It was like time slowed down. Then she locked eyes with me. On her face appeared the same look of horror she had had when I woke up after the accident.

She backed away from the dog that was still barking at her and started walking away with her head down. She was walking so suspiciously fast she might as well have been running.

I watched her take a few steps back, and then my freeze response had shifted into a flight response; before I knew it I just started running. Even though she was walking away from me, and still on the other side of the road, I felt I had to move, to run away. I sprinted to Better Beans, ignoring how running still hurt my fragile hip, and rushed inside. One of my co-workers saw me come in and looked at me from behind the counter.

"Are you okay, Junie?"

I must have looked out of my mind. I had huge bags under my eyes. My skin had been breaking out. I was in my sweats with a dirty hoodie and on top of that, I was now panicked, panting and sweating. I had run, as if my life depended on it, into a calm, serene little coffeehouse where bubbly music was always playing and it always smelled like pies.

Besides my worried co-worker there were several customers giving me weird looks.

"I-I guess, sorry, rough morning," I said, and sat down at a table in a corner.

"Okay," Vienna, my co-worker said, still looking worried. She finished cleaning something behind the counter and walked up to me. "What happened?" she asked softly, as she sat down across from me.

"I, uhm, had a flashback," I said, while avoiding eye contact.

That wasn't the truth, I knew it was real, but I didn't want to have to explain the whole situation, and I would probably not be believed anyway.

"Oh, honey, from the accident?" Vienna asked sympathetically. I nodded. "It must be so hard for you. You know we're all here for you, right? Well, Ian said you might be coming in, so tell me what you want and I'll bring it to you."

I nodded again. "A hummus bagel and a chocolate muffin please," I mumbled with a forced smile.

She brought them over to me a few minutes later with a large glass of freshly squeezed juice. I enjoyed my free breakfast, sure, but I could not stop thinking about what had just happened. Who was this girl? Why was she at the crash? Why had I started having these nightmares? Why was she always in them? And why did she look mortified once again while locking eyes with me?

Chapter Three
Down the Rabbit Hole

All through the weekend, and the days following, my anxiety was through the roof and my nightmares had become even worse.

I was sitting at my friends' apartment one afternoon for the first time after the accident. I had managed to find the courage to go there and spend time with them, but it seemed as if I could barely focus on them. My friend group consisted of my cousin Davin, my friend Callista – whom I had considered my best friend ever since high school and who was coincidentally Davin's girlfriend – and their roommate Stellan. Stellan and Davin had been friends ever since elementary school and had decided to get an apartment together after enrolling at the same university, Callista moved in later.

The three of them lived together in a decent sized apartment on the second floor in a quiet part of town. The apartment was well kept, modern and had been full of plants and flowers ever since Callista had moved in.

I was sitting on the couch in the living room with Dasch's (Stellan's dog) square head on my lap. My friends were all talking but I couldn't help but zone out.

She was in town, I kept thinking. It was all I had been thinking about ever since Friday morning.

"Junie!" said Davin suddenly, his deep voice snapping me out of my overthinking. "I asked if you wanted some pancakes. Stellan's making those wildly good chocolate chip pancakes. You know, the ones that are somehow still healthy."

I quickly looked around and realized that I hadn't even noticed Stellan who was sitting next to me getting up. I simply nodded.

"Okay, I'll go give him a hand then," he said as he got up from sitting next to Callista.

Callista scooted closer to me. "Are you okay, Junie?" she asked me with a look of concern.

"I don't know," I answered honestly.

"Why, what's wrong?"

I looked at her, with the desire to spill it all, about the nightmares, the anxiety, the girl, and the weird feeling I'd had in my stomach ever since I laid eyes on her again, but I couldn't.

About a week or so later, a week of not working but ruminating, obsessing, and feeling odd instead, I decided that I had had enough and that I had to find her. I told myself that this was the way; not talking it over with people who I knew I could confide in, no – I was still telling myself that this woman was just a regular woman who had no intention of harming me, and that if I could just find her, and see it for myself, I could just let it go. Everything would go back to normal and I could go back to just living my life as I had been doing before the accident. I could do this myself. I wouldn't have to bother anyone anymore. They had done enough.

I started by attempting to write a plan. I wrote down the location and time of the accident, the location and time I had seen her in the street and any other information I could come up with.

I wrote down what she had looked like both times, what direction she was walking in the last time; and then something occurred to me that I thought might be helpful.

The second time I had faced her, while walking to the coffeehouse, she had had a bag on her arm – not a bag like a purse, but a plastic bag – a bag from a store. I didn't recognize the design and I also didn't remember any text, but it was a standout design, full of colours and prints, and I figured I would recognize it if I saw it again. *This could be something*, I thought.

I wrote down the details: the size of the bag (small), the colours of the bag (black and neon blue, pink, red and yellow), the type of prints (plaid and checkers) and that it was plastic material, and so the next day I set out to find the store it had come from.

That day I was living on autopilot. I was anxious, short of breath and my chest hurt, more than the usual amount, but I was determined to figure it all out and find her, so I tried to ignore the pain. I was in survival mode.

I stomped down the street to the centre of town, which was not too far from where I lived, barely further than my walk to the coffee shop. On arriving, I started eyeing the stores that had only just opened since it was so early in the morning. I did not want to waste a second.

I didn't recognize anything in this street, so I decided to continue on to the next street, hoping that the store I was looking for was actually in town and it hadn't just been some random bag she had with her.

Luckily, I didn't have to search much. As I walked up the second shopping street my eyes immediately fell on a store whose front had the exact same colours and prints as the bag the nightmare woman had been carrying. I didn't even bother to read the name of the store as I rushed inside.

It was a small, alternative style store; one that I had never really bothered to go into …

There was hard rock music playing and there was band merchandise – racks and racks of it. I saw a glass display with things like hair dye, extensions, contact lenses and jewellery. There were shelves upon shelves with shoes and there were some skateboards and CDs. There was a man behind the counter busy on a laptop while nodding along to the music that was playing. There were no customers inside. After a brief analysis of the store, my eyes fell on a bunch of plastic bags that were hanging by the counter. They were the same bags as the one she had. I knew I had found the right place.

However, I didn't really know what to do next. I couldn't just wait there for hours, hoping she'd walk in. I wasn't even sure if she'd come back here again.

What if she had just randomly been visiting Cunabula both times I saw her and she didn't even live here? What was I to do? Come back here every day, buying stuff I didn't even need, just so I didn't seem too suspicious, hoping I would run into her one day? I sighed, pretended to look through some band shirts and then I walked out again.

I noticed that across from the store was a small bench and I walked over and sat down. On the lamppost a few feet away from where I was sitting was a missing persons poster with both the missing boy and the elderly woman on it. I couldn't bear to pay much attention to it.

I just stared at the store gloomily, unsure of what to do. I must have sat there for a good half hour before I decided to go back home. On my way home I concluded that all I really *could* do was wait and just hope she'd visit the store again. It seemed like a long shot, but I was going to take the chance.

I started sitting on the bench across from the store every single day. Apparently the store was named Checkers. They must really like that print, I thought. It was on their bags, the wallpaper and on the tons of shoes they sold there too.

I brought food with me every time I went to sit on the bench so it would look like I was sitting there with a purpose other than what could probably be classified as stalking a woman.

At this point, I had to tell my boss that I'd had a relapse and needed more time to recover, which luckily, he understood and accepted, but the price I had to pay for lying was the daily fear of running into him or a co-worker every time I was on bench duty.

I figured if that were to happen I'd lie and tell them I came here only to get some fresh air, but the idea still made me nervous. Of course, I also had to dodge Stellan and Dasch when they were out on a walk, a run or a bike ride from time to time. I had lately been avoiding him and the others.

I had barely been outside, let alone meeting up with my friends, only seeing them when they loyally came over to help me out. However, when they did come, it wasn't very convivial. I would do my best not to show that I wanted them to leave as soon as possible but it seemed as if I wasn't doing a very good job at that.

They didn't stick around much longer than they had to, and it seemed as if they felt like they didn't have much choice.

I went to the bench at different times every day, figuring that it would give me the best chance of catching her some time. I secretly admitted to myself that all of it had become an obsession.

It took almost a whole month of obsessively lurking on that bench, neglecting myself, my house and my social life, before I spotted her again. Initially I panicked when I saw her. She *did* almost run away when she saw me the last time. I knew that if she saw me my effort would have been for nothing. She'd leave before I got the chance to talk to her.

So, when I finally saw her walk up to the store, and before she had the chance to see me, I rushed into another store to hide from her gaze.

I was now standing in a random clothing store while adrenaline pumped through my veins. I peeked through the display windows to see if she went into Checkers, and she did. She hadn't seen me. Now I just had to wait until she came back out and then confront her. I had no idea what I was going to say as we had never said a word to each other, but it just felt like something I had to do.

To avoid looking like a fugitive, I greeted the employees at the clothing store and started looking through the racks of clothing. I kept close to the windows so I could look up as often as possible to see if she went back out. It probably took less than two minutes before she did.

I watched her as she walked out of the store, this time without a bag it seemed, and down the street. I almost flew out of the store.

"Wait!" I blurted out.

She turned back, looking at me from across the street, awaiting my response. There was that mortified expression again.

"You-you were at my accident!" I stuttered, as I walked up to her. The odd feeling in my stomach was starting to come back again.

She blinked a few times and her expression changed to confusion.

"Remember me? I was in a car accident five months ago. I saw you."

I was now standing next to her. It took a few seconds for her to react, and then her expression changed once again.

"Oh, of course I remember you! What happened was horrific. I'm glad to see you're doing okay," she said, and gave me a warm smile.

The energy she gave off was a complete one eighty-degree reversal from the fear that had been installed in me by my nightmares. I could see that she was eager to continue walking. I had to quickly continue talking to keep her attention.

"Did you wake me up?" I blurted. "Did you call an ambulance? Why were you there?"

"I called the ambulance, yes. I happened to be nearby."

"Oh, well, thank you," I concluded. I didn't really know what to say now that I was speaking to her and her seemed to be perfectly fine. I guess I had fulfilled my quest.

"Are you okay? You seem ... like you've just seen a ghost," she said, and squinted a bit.

"I, uhm, yeah. I'm okay."

"Good," she said and smiled again. "Well, I've got to go, it was nice to meet you conscious and well. Stay safe."

"I'm Junie," I blurted as she started turning around again. I stuck out my hand for her to shake.

"Bluebell," she said as the turned back and shook my hand with her gloved one. Her handshake felt awfully stiff.

I tried to think of a quick way to stop her from leaving. I wasn't sure why. "Would you like to go for lunch or something? It's on me. I feel like I owe you."

She laughed. "You don't owe me anything! I would love to, but I really shouldn't. I have somewhere to go."

"Please?" I squeaked, out of ideas now. She looked a little startled, or did I catch a bit of annoyance?

"Uhm, okay, I guess I can shuffle some things around. I just ate though so don't stuff me," she said, and winked.

We both laughed and I led the way to a little lunch place nearby.

Chapter Four

Redrum

The lunch was going well, but there were also more questions rising in my head than I previously had. Bluebell seemed to be a really nice person. She had been really empathetic towards my struggles, to the point where it seemed to almost hurt *her* a bit. She didn't eat much. She didn't seem to want to talk about herself much either. I attributed it to her being somewhat socially awkward. It didn't seem as if she had lunch with people often. However, she was a good listener.

What hadn't stood out to me before was that Bluebell looked rather rough from up close. She had beautiful blue eyes, though; that was undeniable. Red, wavy hair up to a little above her shoulders.

Her nose was unusual. It was crooked and scarred, like someone had hit her on the nose hard enough to break it several times, with something other than just a fist, because that wouldn't explain the scarring. She also had scars on her lip that looked as if she had suffered cuts there.

Overall, her face seemed as if it had seen some rough times. Her skin was pale to the point that it looked unhealthy, and she was painfully thin. Bluebell herself seemed harmless, soothing my fears a little, but from the looks of her it seemed as if she might herself be in some danger. I had been afraid to ask, as I didn't know how to bring up such a thing on our first meeting.

She was wearing a t-shirt, which was weird as it was unusually cold for a late summer's day. She had those gloves on her hands. Overall, there was something odd about her, but it didn't show in the way she spoke.

"Would you like anything else?" our waiter asked when we finished our food, ignoring an extremely annoying fly that had been bugging us, especially Bluebell, the whole time.

"A green tea for me please," I answered. "No honey, please."

I looked up at Bluebell, who still looked as awkward as she had when we sat down.

"Me too," she added. She had only eaten a small cupcake and had had nothing to drink yet. The waiter nodded and went on his way.

"Any other plans for today?" I asked, trying to make conversation.

"Actually, I have to start packing, I'm going away for a bit."

"Oh," I said, feeling a little disappointed for some reason. "Where to?"

"Invicta."

"Wow," I said in disbelief, "that's not a small trip."

Invicta was a country hours and hours away from Aspera.

She smiled. I noticed she had perfect teeth. "I have family there that I need to go see. It's been a while."

"That's awesome, do you go there often?"

She shook her head. "They mostly visit me here, so it's a nice change."

Our tea came, and we thanked the waiter.

"So, what's your family's relation to Invicta?" I asked curiously.

"They love the food there," she joked. "No, they do, but they just love the country, and they feel at home there. One day they just moved and never looked back."

We drank our tea and talked a little about travelling which Bluebell seemed to have done a lot of. She was born here in Aspera but had travelled everywhere one might want to go to and she had lived in quite a few places too.

I couldn't wrap my head around how a girl who couldn't have been much older than me had found the time and money to do all that, but I didn't ask. I did find out that she was also living in Cunabula, so I figured I'd see her around more often.

After we drank our tea, I went to the bathroom and Bluebell, who had offered, paid the bill.

The fly had stopped zooming around the table at last, and now sat on a small plant. When I came back to the table a moment later, I caught a very annoyed look on Bluebell's face, before her expression quickly changed when she saw I had returned.

"Ready?" she asked warmly. I nodded and we got up. I grabbed a napkin from the table.

As we walked out, the fly went out with us and disappeared at last.

We shared some small talk outside the café. She told me she hoped I'd feel better soon, and I wished her good travels. Before we said our goodbyes, however, I couldn't hold myself back any longer ...

"I just wanted to ask ... Are you okay? I don't know what your living situation is but if you need someone to talk to, feel free to reach out to me." I quickly scribbled down my phone number on the napkin that I had taken from the café and handed it to her.

She smiled at me, but it seemed rather forced. "Thank you, that's really nice," was all she said.

We shook hands one last time and went our separate ways. Feeling relieved, although still having that odd sensation in my stomach, I made my way home contentedly.

Later that day, I lay down on my couch going over the lunch we had had earlier in my head. I hadn't mentioned anything about the nightmares or about why I was afraid of her. I hadn't asked her why she had looked so startled when she saw me. She never asked me why I was so eager to talk to her and had practically yelled at her in the middle of the street, which I thought was a bit odd.

It had been a very pleasant lunch though, despite her seeming a bit uneasy. The way she looked was still on my mind. She looked as if she'd been held captive without sunlight or food for a long time and hadn't slept during that time either; and the scars on her face and the broken nose ... I tried to get it out of my head, reminding myself that I had given her a way to reach me if she needed to and that I had done what I could.

I stared out the window into the sunset and finally took the time to come to terms with the feeling I'd been having since I had seen her on the street that particular Friday. It was a weird type of uneasiness, but it was also pleasant. It wasn't as intense as it had been during the lunch, or when we locked eyes on the street. It seemed to be fading away a bit now. I wondered if I had been having this feeling all those months while I had been recovering too. Was it really new or had I just not realized it until now?

I spent the rest of the night thinking about Bluebell, concluding that whatever I was feeling, everything now would return to normal. She was normal. Everything was fine.

That mind-set came to an end when I woke up covered in sweat in the middle of the night from a nightmare that had been even worse than any of the ones I'd been having for months.

It started with me and Bluebell having lunch again and just like before, I came back to Bluebell sitting at our table alone. This time I didn't catch an annoyed expression on her face but saw that she had turned into a monster. Before I had the time to react, she lunged at me and killed me.

The fact that I had died in my dreams was nothing new but Bluebell suddenly becoming a monster *was* new and dying in the dream felt terrifyingly real. It felt as if my soul had been sucked out of my body and when I woke up, my body still wasn't feeling right.

I started to notice that my body was actually aching, not as badly as in the dream – I didn't think that could happen – but it did hurt. I took one of the many painkillers that were still on my nightstand and lay back down. Despite it being Bluebell who had hurt me in my nightmare I wished I could talk to her. She had been so understanding ... I wondered if she'd be understanding if I told her all of this. I sighed and secretly wished I had taken her number too.

The next morning, I woke up to a check-up phone call from my mum. When it rang, I grabbed it as fast as I could but was disappointed to see that it wasn't Bluebell.

After talking to my mum, I sat down to have breakfast, but I felt empty. I had met the person who had been haunting me, but I didn't feel as good as I thought I would have.

I still had the nightmares, my body ached; I was still anxious and on top of that a new type of restlessness had found its way to me. I couldn't really put my finger on it.

For some distraction, I turned on the television and unlucky for my anxiety there was another breaking news story. I turned up the volume so I could hear it properly through the crunching of my granola. I listened closely.

"This just in, the body of a …"

Did they find the boy? Did they find the lady?

"A three year old girl has been found in Cunabula town centre just outside a local lunchroom. On site we have a police spokesman …"

The screen cut to an interviewer and a policeman standing outside the lunchroom I had visited with Bluebell yesterday. There was police tape everywhere and a white tent. I felt the earth drop out from underneath me and it seemed as if I were in a movie. Then my phone rang again.

This time I *was* expecting my mum, who worked for the police, but it was an unknown caller.

"Junie?" a familiar voice asked. "Hi, I was just watching the news, have you seen it?"

It was her. Bluebell was calling me.

"Y-yeah, I'm watching it now," I answered, trembling slightly.

"I just wanted to check in and see if you were okay."

"Yes, I'm fine, thank you for asking," I answered, zoned out and *not* feeling okay.

"What stands out is the obscure condition that the toddler was found in. What could possibly have happened here, sir?" the interviewer asked the policeman, on the news. I wasn't present enough to hear the answer.

"Just be careful out there, okay, Junie? Maybe stay inside until they have figured out more."

I nodded and then realized that she obviously couldn't see me.

"Y-yes, I will. Do you maybe …"

"I've got to go now, Invicta, remember? Stay safe, you can reach me here. Bye."

She hung up before I got the chance to ask her to come over.

I put my phone down in slow motion, anxiety rushed through my veins. I took a deep breath and then walked over to the couch and lay down.

This town is going to shit, I thought to myself.

It dawned on me that if somebody had murdered a helpless baby, it was likely that the missing boy and elderly lady had met the same fate but just hadn't been found yet.

Could there really be a serial killer in a town like Cunabula? … It felt surreal. Having a mother who did detective work, and having a degree in criminal justice myself, I didn't expect to feel so startled, but I did. Over the last months it had started to feel as if death was after me and my fascination for the macabre, and my interest in crime were fading away. I wanted nothing to do with it.

I wondered about the possible serial killer, though; were they becoming less careful or were they trying to provoke the public by leaving a dead body inside the town centre like that? Why? What did they want? And what kind of coward targets the helpless?

It wasn't until around noon when I found out the condition that the body had been found in.

On the phone again with my mum, I was told that the body of the infant was found completely dried out. There were no fluids, no blood … It was barely a corpse. It was just a bag of bones and shrivelled organs. It sounded as if a gigantic spider had gotten hold of the girl.

In all her years working for the police my mother had never encountered anything like it. There were also bite marks all over the tiny girl's body.

My dad, who worked in psychology, had theorized that the killer was possibly having an episode where they thought they were some kind of monster that sucked blood, like a spider, a bat or at the further end of severity, a vampire.

Whatever it was, with the two disappearances and now a confirmed murder, Cunabula had become an unsafe place to live in in a very short period of time.

My mother worked overtime because the murder and disappearances were considered possibly connected, since all three people under inspection were fairly vulnerable.

The detectives on the case wanted to be prepared for a worst-case scenario; it was possible the two missing people had already been murdered too.

There was only one thing that kept me sane and that was the thought that I wasn't helpless, and neither were my family or my friends, so I took that as comfort and I only hoped that there would be no more disappearances or murder victims, especially not healthy individuals – for my own sake.

Chapter Five

Rock Bottom

Barely a week later, my last bit of comfort slipped away from me. There had been another murder in town. This time it was not someone terminally ill, it was not a senior citizen or a child that something had happened to; it was an adult woman around my age with no apparent health problems, and she was dead. She was last seen leaving her workplace at night and was found dead the next morning.

Shrivelled, dehydrated, bite marks all over her, no blood left in her body. Just a dried-out bag of what was once a woman. She was left in the same state as the toddler had been in.

The whole town was terrified and no one could explain how it happened.

Even if one believed they were a bloodsucking monster, how would they go about draining every last bit of blood from a person's body? And where would it go?

My exhausted mother didn't have the answers either. At the station they were still working overtime but had no leads whatsoever. There was no DNA found and there were no clues. My father had been busier at his job too: the practice he worked at was the only psychological help available in town and on top of the loved ones of the victims, more and more people started feeling unsafe now that their town had become home to a serial killer. I had stopped accepting my parents' help; they were busy enough. I had also stopped accepting the help from my friends, even while they had the best intentions, their company only made me feel worse … They were all so … happy; doing so well.

It made me feel worse about myself. I didn't have much time to ruminate over any of it, however.

On the Wednesday night, exhausted as they were, my parents had invited me over to have a talk with them. It took place over a delicious dinner of hearty stew made with lentils and squash. After a fair bit of small talk and catching up, my father laid it on me.

"Junie, darling, we wanted to ... offer you some help."

"Yes, dear, we feel that you might be relapsing. You haven't been working, Davin told us you practically cut off contact with your friends ... Your house is a mess and well, frankly, you look a mess too."

It was true. Not even a year ago I had my life together, working at a job I liked, keeping a tidy home and taking care of myself. Everything was going well. Now ... I was lucky to still be on paid leave, but I spent all my time in a house filled with piled-up dust and trash from take-out food, which simultaneously was draining my bank account. My hair was neglected. My skin looked a mess – the deep brown now interrupted by splotches and pimples, the bags under my eyes could have their own brand and I had lost a noticeable amount of weight. It was unlike me, but I couldn't keep up anymore.

"We feel it might be good for you to start seeing Doctor Stewart again," added my father. "He's told me before that you'd be more than welcome if you needed more help."

'Doctor Stewart', aka Donald, as he told me to call him, was the shrink I had been seeing after the accident. He helped me a great deal with recovery and was a great therapist. If I were to go back to him, I just had to make sure to leave out the part where I had almost lost my mind over a person I didn't know, let alone the stalking and now having her phone number ...

I nodded to my dad. "That may be helpful. I was doing better but ... everything that has been going on hasn't really helped my anxiety."

My mother smiled faintly.

"I'll let him know tomorrow," said my dad, a look of gratefulness crossing his stubbly face.

"We also worry that the stress of work might not be helpful," my mother chimed in. "I know you love it there, honey, but maybe it's best for you if you don't have to worry about that for a while."

"You mean quit?"

She looked down, playing with her food. "It's been six months, Junie, and you've barely been able to work at all. Eventually they are going to run out of patience for the sake of their business. Maybe it's best to not have that pressure on you."

I looked down at my own food. She was right. I had no idea how long it would take for me to pull myself back together, especially at a time like this where nothing felt safe anymore. I'd been working at the coffeehouse for three years already and I loved it there … but the present situation couldn't go on forever.

"Right," I said sadly. I had accepted the fact, "but how will I get by?"

My parents both let out a little laugh as if I said something bizarre. "Junie, you know better than to think your folks would just let you do it all by yourself," said my dad. "We talked about it, and we thought that maybe you could stay with us until you get back on your feet."

A smile of relief appeared on my face. The thought of that felt like a weight had been lifted off my shoulders.

I thought it over for a few days and eventually decided that my parents were indeed right. I scheduled an appointment with Donald the shrink and went to my workplace to tell them I would be resigning. My co-workers were sad but understanding. Ian looked as if he had his heart broken but also assured me that he understood and wished me all the best, and if I ever wanted to come back and they were looking to hire, I wouldn't even have to go through the whole process.

I walked out of there feeling melancholy but relieved and walked to the nearby bus stop to go to my parents' place. They told me they would take care of my house, move my stuff over and end my lease, much to my relief.

All the change would normally have been a huge stress factor but at that point I was happy to go back to a place where I felt safe and knew I'd be taken care of.

The bus ride was no longer than fifteen minutes, but it felt like forever on that particular day. I was desperate to just go back to bed and spend the day doing absolutely nothing. And that was exactly what I did.

The next day was my appointment with Donald. When my dad had brought it up it had seemed a great idea, but now that I had to go, I wished I would have declined. I had to drag myself out of bed, force feed myself breakfast and it took all the energy in my body to put on decent clothing. It was walking distance from my parents' house to the clinic my dad and Donald worked at, but it felt like a marathon. The worst part of it all was the appointment itself. I had to lie continuously. Being good at his job as he was, Donald could tell from the get-go that there was more to the story than I had been letting on.

I had to lie about the nightmares, lie that nothing else had been happening and only minutes into the session I realized that therapy didn't work like that. It seemed hopeless.

Upon returning home, I threw myself onto my bed and immediately started crying into my pillow. I felt so alone. My mental health was terrible. Therapy was not going to work and now I had no job, which threw my future plans to move away out of the window, and with no house to live in now I had nothing going for myself. I couldn't talk to my parents in detail about how I was feeling, as much as they wanted me to, and I didn't want to talk to any of my friends either … At that moment it dawned on me that maybe there was someone I *did* want to talk to about all of it. I could talk to Bluebell, couldn't I? I was sure you could still make phone calls from Invicta. I reached for my phone, pretended not to see Callista's messages and dialled Bluebell's number. I could talk to her about nightmares from the accident, she'd understand. She didn't have to know that they always involved her, right?

But Bluebell didn't pick up. So I tried again. Still no luck. I sighed and turned onto my side, looking out of my old bedroom window into the unusually rainy street.

That would be the thing that filled most of my days from there on out. Fall was coming.

Chapter Six

Devlin

The days seemed to be getting even longer after I moved in with my parents and the nights felt as if time stood still.

I had absolutely nothing useful to do. The only reason I left the house was to go and lie to Donald and once to pick up cigarettes from the grocery store. I had never been a big smoker, only sometimes accepting a cigarette from someone who was trying to be kind in the odd way of offering me one when I seemed to be under stress; so, it had become a logical thing to do when things got rough. This was one of those times.

The constant sweating in my short windows of sleep – filled with nightmares – mixed with the daytime sweating from general anxiety, combined with cigarette smoke and the fact that showering had become more of a luxury than a necessity made for a stench around me worse than the depressing energy I was giving off. My skin looked like a battlefield and my hair had completely dried out. I moved slow and everything felt heavy. At times I wondered if it would've been better if I had just died in the accident. This was no way to live, and I couldn't think of a possible way to get back to a life that was worth living. I didn't want to talk about it with anyone who asked, and the one person I wanted to talk to still wouldn't answer my calls, for some reason that hurt on a whole different level.

One particularly chilly night, I couldn't just sit in my room anymore and actually found myself near a bridge just outside of town. I was just sitting down on the ground staring at it, contemplating whether I should just do it. The thought didn't make me feel sad. I felt nothing. Nothing whatsoever. The only thing I did feel was a strange physical force that was drawing me to the bridge as if it were reaching out to me.

I decided to just walk up there. As I did, all I could think of was about how freeing it would be to just jump and never having to deal with these horrors of nightmares again, never having to spend another day just staring into nothing – unable to do anything else, never having to worry about being ignored by Bluebell again, although I still wasn't sure why that hurt so much, never having to be in this murder town again … I found myself next to the way up to the bridge. Just staring at it, contemplating.

It felt like something beyond myself made me break the stare and start walking towards it when –

"Hello there," sounded from behind me.

I froze in my tracks and slowly turned around. It must have been around midnight and the last thing I was expecting was to have somebody sneak up on me.

I locked eyes with a young, tall man and to my horror the first thing that stood out to me was that his eyes were completely white. There was no colour, no pupil, nothing at all.

He was casually leaning against a tree, looking like he was longing for something. I backed up instinctively.

"Now, now, don't leave," he said as he took a step forward. "We just met."

He opened his lips to reveal an extremely creepy smile. The smile only made him look worse combined with those colourless, dead eyes.

"Get away from me," I pushed out of my clenched teeth.

His smile got even bigger. "Why would I do that? You've set such a perfect scene for me; I wouldn't dare let it go to waste."

All I could think about was that this clearly deranged man was about to rape me. I held on to the thought that I had my keys in my pocket and that could be my defence. I started to back away a little more.

"If you let me go now, we can forget all about this. You don't have to do this," I said, trying to negotiate with him.

37

He raised a thick eyebrow and snickered. "Always the same with you people."

It sounded like he pronounced the last word with some kind of mocking tone to it. It fit his bratty voice and he continuously sounded like a bullying, taunting child.

"I'm not going to violate you, woman. There's something else I need."

His disturbing smile appeared again. He started slowly pacing forward, still smiling, and the closer he got the clearer I could see how filthy he looked. His clothes were ragged and looked ancient, his blond hair looked like it hadn't seen a brush in ages and his mouth was extraordinarily dirty. There were pieces and smudges of red and brown everywhere. The last thing I noticed made my skin crawl and my heart sink to my stomach. His canine teeth were a good size up from those of any human I ever saw. I instantly connected it to the murders that had been committed … and the victims' bodies that had been sucked dry. I grabbed my keys and held them in front of me as a threat.

"I don't know why you're doing this but you're not gonna get away with it. It's not too late to stop."

He stopped in his tracks and just started laughing uncontrollably while looking at my keys.

"You are a funny one, did you know that?" he asked after finally composing himself, "with your little keys. I appreciate the good laugh but let's get to business now."

He was coming closer and closer and it would have been intimidating enough having a man a head taller than me closing up on me like this, had he had normal eyes and teeth, but he didn't.

Within the blink of an eye, he pulled the keys out of my hand and threw them away out of sight.

I swallowed nervously and backed into one of the pillars of the bridge.

He was closing in on me now, and for some reason sniffed the air as he did so, a satisfied look on his face.

"Get away from her," a familiar voice said firmly. The man stopped in his tracks and turned around with an expression of disgust and annoyance. Behind him, next to the tree he had been leaning against, stood Bluebell!

"Get lost," she said.

"*You!*" he spat, accusingly, somehow still sounding like a little boy with a raspy voice. "Get lost yourself."

"She belongs to me."

There was silence for a moment when he turned back towards me.

"Is that so?" he grinned and started scanning me with his eyes. "Better hurry then, she looks she hasn't eaten in a good while."

"Go."

He looked me up and down one last time and then swiftly started walking away.

I couldn't help but fall to my knees. It was like I had lost all strength in my limbs. Bluebell rushed over to me and knelt next to me.

"You need to go home. It's not safe out." I nodded, unable to speak. She helped me up. "Where do you live?"

"Apricus Passage ..." I mumbled.

Bluebell didn't respond, she just held me up and we started walking towards Apricus Passage. It was a fairly long walk but I remembered none of it by the time I arrived at the front door. I just started to realize that I had no keys when the door swung open and my mum threw her arms around me.

"Junie, we were so worried! It happened again!"

My father was standing behind her, a look of joyful relief on his face. His dark brown eyes looked tired.

"Come in, darling. Let's get you warmed up."

My mum let go of me and turned to Bluebell. "Thank you for bringing her home!"

"Oh, yeah, this is, uhm, my friend Bluebell," I quickly said.

Both my parents shook her hand and gave her a look of appreciation.

"Oh my, you're freezing too," my mother said as she shook her hand. "Would you like to come in too?"

"I, uhm ..."

"It's not safe out, who knows what might happen!" said my father.

"I ..."

"Come," I said, noticing the look of uncertainty on Bluebell's face.

"Yeah! Come on in!" My mother pretty much pulled me and Bluebell inside, and then closed and firmly locked the door behind us.

Within what seemed like seconds, my father made us both tea and my parents sat down across from us.

"Where *were* you, Junie?" My father couldn't help himself, his question full of worry.

"I, uhm, I was taking a walk," I stumbled out.

"In the middle of the night?! Especially in these times, what were you ..."

"Yes, that's why she was with me, sir. She said she needed to take a walk but didn't want to go alone so we went together," Bluebell chimed in.

I gave her a grateful look. I had a feeling that she knew exactly what I was trying to do there.

"Well, that was a good choice, but still, this is very dangerous. You could both have been hurt!"

"I'm just so glad you're all right. Thank you again," my mother said, as she nodded at Bluebell.

I wanted to leave it at that and just go to bed but I didn't get my way.

"If you don't mind me asking, ma'am, you said that it happened again, did you mean ...?" Bluebell asked.

My mother nodded. "I only just got the call. A woman in her twenties. The first thing we did was to look for Junie but she wasn't there ..."

Bluebell just nodded but it only then started to sink into me. It *could* have been me and it probably would have been if Bluebell hadn't shown up. I started going over the situation in my head and started to realize what an odd situation it had been.

"That reminds me, I have to get to the station," my mum said, as she sprang up and hastily started looking around for her purse.

"Wait," I said, much to the surprise of everyone else. "I think I can help."

My mother started sitting back down, her made-up eyes looking suspicious. "What do you mean?"

I looked at Bluebell, who was looking at the table in front of her with sudden great interest.

"I think we saw the person who is behind all this."

My parents both looked at me with horror. From the corner of my eye, I saw Bluebell give me a similar look. My mother pulled a notebook and a pen out of nowhere and gave me a strict look.

"We were ... walking near the big bridge, on the underside, and we came across a man."

"What did he look like?"

"Regular physique, kind of tall ... He had blond hair, very dirty and uncombed. He was white, very pale. And ..." I had to pause for a second, "I know this may sound odd, but his eyes were white."

"His eyes were white?" my mum asked with raised eyebrows.

I nodded. "There was no pupil. No colour, nothing."

"Okay ..." my mum said as she wrote it all down.

"And his mouth was ... disgusting. There was filth everywhere. Pieces of meat, blood. Like he had been eating raw meat or something. And he seemed to have ... fangs. Like a ... a big cat, or a wolf or something."

My mother was still writing everything down eagerly. "Sounds very alarming ... He must have gotten contacts and fake fangs or some sort of body modification ... What kind of clothes was he wearing?"

"I don't know ... just regular clothes, a shirt and pants. The pants were black I think, a shirt with some sort of print, sneakers, but they were very dirty too. Maybe he is homeless or something, I don't know. It was pretty cold for walking around in a T-shirt."

"Did he have facial hair?"

"No, nothing …"

"What age would you estimate him to be?"

"Maybe nineteen, twenty."

My mum nodded. "Did anything else stand out?"

"No, not really …"

At that point a scary thought popped into my head; he seemed to know Bluebell. I quickly looked over at her and she was still looking surprised, or scared more so, but she quickly tried to hide it as soon as I looked over at her. She very slowly shook her head.

"But that was it, really. He said he wanted something from me but pointed out that he didn't want to violate me, and he was oddly calm."

I gave Bluebell a suspicious side-eye.

My mother finished writing and then looked up at me, awaiting more information.

"That's all I got, Mum."

"All right dear, if you remember anything else, let me know. Same goes for you," she said as she pointed her pen at Bluebell. She placed her hands in her kinky hair, closed her eyes for a moment and took a deep breath, and then started to get up again.

"Let's get you to bed," my father chimed in, as he saw my mum preparing to go to work.

My mother thanked Bluebell one last time and then went out.

My dad nodded at me, and we started getting up. I looked awkwardly at Bluebell, who was still there, in a house that was strange to her.

"Would you like to stay over?" my father asked while looking at her.

Bluebell seemed puzzled. "I shouldn't, I don't live that far from here, I'll be okay," she assured him, much to my relief, as I was not keen to have someone in the house who I started to realize had some sort of connection to a possible murderer.

"I insist. You can't go out there by yourself and I'm not letting Junie go outside again or stay here by herself. You can stay in the guestroom."

Bluebell still looked puzzled, clearly looking for a reason not to stay, but my dad wouldn't let her go.

"Come," he said as he led the way to the stairs. We both followed him, to my disappointment, and to Bluebell's, seemingly.

We went up and my dad showed her the guestroom, wished us good night and went back downstairs. Before Bluebell had the chance to say or do anything I stepped in front of her and closed the door behind us.

"Would you like to tell me what that was all about?!" I spat, trying to keep my voice down.

She looked mortified, a look that I had become familiar with now. She opened her mouth and it looked like she was trying to think of something to say but she couldn't think of anything.

Eventually her whole demeanour changed, and she sighed. She became less tense, moved me out of the way and locked the door behind us.

"Sit," she said.

"Excuse me?"

"Please?" she said, rather impatiently.

I gave her a look but sat down on the bed anyway.

"You have to promise me you won't tell anyone," she said firmly.

I raised my eyebrows. "Okay ..." I said hesitantly.

"The bridge guy and I are sort of ... related," she said, as though it wasn't quite the right word but the best one she could come up with.

"Related?! How?!"

"Distant, but we don't get along very well. We're very different."

I believed the part about not getting along. He had seemed to loathe the fact that she was even near him.

"Why?"

"We have different values," she answered vaguely.

"What sort of values?"

"Just listen, Junie. He is just not a good person. You have to promise me ..."

"*Promise you?!* You literally ran from me, then you act like you're my friend but disappear to Invicta, ignoring all of my attempts to contact you, then you turn up in the middle of the night to save me from your deranged ... cousin or something and you want to talk about promises?!"

"Shhhh!"

"Don't you tell me what to do or I swear to I'll ..."

She walked up to me and knelt in front of me and looked me in the eyes. "Junie, I know none of this makes sense to you, but can you believe me when I say that I'm trying to protect you?"

"Protect me? You?"

"Yes, but I can't tell you why. I already said too much. I need you to keep this to yourself at all costs, can you do that?"

I nodded slightly.

"You have to promise me to not get involved in this case. It's not safe."

"It's not safe? Case ... Do you mean that he ...?"

Her silence and dead stare confirmed what I was thinking.

"If you ever see that guy again, or if you start dreaming ..." My heart dropped to my stomach, and I instinctively backed away. She grabbed my wrists and kept looking me in the eye, a bit too intensely for my taste. "If you start dreaming about someone else, having nightmares, you have to let me know right away." Then she let me go and backed away. I could feel my chest tighten and a lump in my throat forming. "Listen, I am not going to hurt you, but I'm not going to try to convince you of that. I'm gonna keep my distance and let you be. But please, if you start having new nightmares, contact me."

I nodded. New nightmares...

She turned around and started walking to the door and unlocked it. "Oh, and if you hear his name anywhere, let me know as well."

She opened the door and stepped away to let me out.

"What is his name?" I asked hesitantly.

"Devlin."

Chapter Seven

The Cemetery

The night after the incident was surprisingly calm, it was the first time in a while I had slept well. Though I thought I heard some voices right outside my window sometime during the night, but being drowsy as I was, I fell asleep before I could think much of it.

It probably wasn't much anyway, I thought to myself the next morning. I went downstairs, and found Bluebell sitting at the table with my father. I guess she was a morning person just like him.

"Good morning," I said. They both greeted me back and my father waved his hand to invite me over to the table.

"How did you sleep?" he asked.

"Good, thank you," I answered. "You?"

"Fine, thank you."

"How about you?" I asked Bluebell.

"Good too," she said and smiled faintly.

"Can I get you some breakfast, Junie? Are you sure you don't want any?" he asked Bluebell. She nodded.

I asked him to just bring a bowl, some oat drink and froot loops. I wasn't in the mood for anything healthy.

Sketchy as the situation with Bluebell was, I was feeling more curious than anything else.

After I finished eating, I went out to fulfil my stress habit of smoking and Bluebell went with me.

"I'm aware," I chuckled as I saw Bluebell's eyes looking at my cigarette, a neutral expression but probably silently judging.

She smiled. "Sorry, I just think it's a shame. Life is fragile."

I nodded. "It is. I cave when I'm too stressed. I don't even like it. Have you ever smoked?"

She shook her head.

"Good." I ended the conversation.

It was silent for a moment, a million questions still running through my head and Bluebell was clearly still not willing to talk about any of it.

"I should go," she said, breaking the silence before it got too awkward, playing with the thin gloves she was wearing again.

"Oh," I said, expecting to be relieved but feeling more disappointed than anything. "I understand. Thank you again, for last night."

She smiled. "No need to thank me. Stay safe."

"Should we hug?" I blurted out before I could stop myself.

"Uhm, okay," she said hesitantly, and smiled awkwardly.

I went in for a brief hug, since she was clearly uncomfortable. We said our goodbyes and she left, leaving me feeling odd and uneasy once again.

Minutes later a familiar face appeared; it was Callista.

"You almost *died,* and you still won't talk to us?!"

I cursed mentally, wondering how on earth she knew about it.

"That's right." She continued, "Davin told me. He's been keeping up with the case through Esther. At least your mother has the decency to speak to us."

"I'm sorry," I mumbled, looking down.

Callista took a deep breath, so deep that her exhale made her bangs fly away from her forehead for a second as she tried to compose herself.

"I'm worried about you, Junie, we all are! Even Dasch misses you. You didn't even tell me you moved out. You didn't tell me you quit your job ..." she said.

"You're the one who took me in when my folks threw me out. Why won't you let me help you?"

"You're right," I admitted. "I'm sorry, Calli."

"I'm not asking for much," she said. "Just answer me occasionally, even if you just want to talk about the weather. We can hang out in silence. It doesn't matter. Just ... don't leave."

Her voice broke as she said the last part and I instinctively went in for a hug. It was a tight, emotional hug, and I had to admit that it felt good, although I couldn't help but think that it didn't feel as good as the brief hug Bluebell and I had just shared.

That night my mother came home from work late, in great distress. She sat down exhausted. When she noticed our curious faces, she simply said, "Watch the news at twelve, I don't want to talk about it anymore."

When it was almost twelve, she left the room and went up to go to bed.

My father and I curiously turned on the TV, not sure what to expect, but we knew it wasn't going to be pretty. My mother had seen many crimes, investigated many murders but she had never dealt with a serial killer before, let alone one in her own town.

Then it came on. There were new developments in the case. We watched quietly as they summed up what had already been discovered and considered and they showed photos of the already confirmed victims: the toddler and the woman in her twenties. But they discovered more.

In a forest just outside of Cunabula, called Tumulo Forest, they had found the bodies of the people who had been missing up until now: the elderly woman and the terminally ill boy. They had been buried, for a while it seemed, but furthermore their bodies were in a similar state as the confirmed murder victims and the cases were now officially connected.

The people hadn't gone missing, they were murdered too; they were inflicted with what looked like bite marks (albeit only a single bite mark, and not tons and tons as had been on the previously confirmed murder victims) and had their blood drained, before they were buried. There was no answer as to why the other two victims had been left out in the street for everyone to see and had so many more wounds. Did the case not get enough attention and was the killer getting impatient when they decided to murder them? Did they change their ways for another reason? The police said there were no clues as to who could've done it. *Perhaps besides Devlin,* I thought.

The other curious part about the find was that buried around the two corpses were hundreds of animal skeletons, from squirrels to house cats to owls to horses. It was a hidden cemetery. Some skeletons had been there for a long time and were mere bones, others were buried more recently and in the same condition as the human victims: drained of fluids and just skin wrapped around bones. There were also older human skeletons of yet to be identified victims.

The forest was now considered a crime scene, and no one was allowed in anymore.

Chapter Eight

Rosabella

After the incident I found myself hanging out a lot with Bluebell, who seemed suddenly to have let go of her distant ways as she never ignored or tried to avoid me anymore. I was trying to regularly answer Callista, and Davin and Stellan, but I still couldn't get myself to physically meet up with them.

Bluebell, however, came over to my parents' house often.

We didn't talk about the incident; we didn't talk about the murders, or the cemetery and we didn't talk about my nightmares or how I continuously felt sad and even anxious every time she left.

She hadn't asked to sleep over again, but it was getting harder and harder to sleep at night now that I, for some reason, also started feeling some sort of … withdrawal, for lack of a better term, whenever she decided to go home. So, I decided to ask her.

Much to my surprise, she agreed without much hesitation and that night I was sleeping like a rock while Bluebell was on a comfortable mattress on the floor next to me. It didn't take me hours to fall asleep and it was solid sleep until I woke up from something external and I found the mattress next to me empty. I sat up and took some time to get myself back to earth when I realized that I had woken up because there were voices outside. They sounded like they were trying to keep it down, but they weren't doing a great job.

I got up and moved closer to my window, doing my best to stay away from it, so whoever it was wouldn't see me standing there to eavesdrop. I closed my eyes and listened carefully when I recognized Bluebell's attempt at whispering.

"I have no choice; they are going to kill her!" she silently screamed.

"Better her than you!" another female voice spat, a little louder. "You can't keep this up! You know how this is gonna end! When will you learn?! Eventually the human is going to die anyway, why would you risk yourself for that?!"

"I am *not* going to let them kill her," Bluebell replied firmly. "It is not an option. This is my fault and she's not taking the fall for that."

"Listen to me," the other voice said, almost threatening, but then changed to a more desperate tone. "We've been over this. Don't you remember last time? She will die and *if* miraculously she survives long enough, *they* will kill her." The voice stopped talking for a moment and then continued. "Ever since you came here, I've been keeping an eye on you. Trying to keep you safe. To protect you from your family. But you know I can't fight them. We could never take them on and you're basically inviting them like this. You know this, Willow. You're putting yourself in danger too."

"I would never ask you to fight them for me, but you also know that I would kill myself right now if I could," she spat. "This is no life. I would gladly die for any human who actually values their life!"

"And you've tried that before but you're still here, aren't you?!"

It was silent for a moment and then I heard footsteps walking towards my window.

I ran back to my bed and got under the blanket as if I never moved. In the blink of an eye, I heard someone come through my window. I peeked and saw Bluebell standing next to it, staring outside. She let out a sigh and lay down on her mattress, now staring at the ceiling.

I decided that it was best to not ask questions at this point as I was clearly not meant to hear any of that, and so I pretended to be asleep. My mind, however, was racing with questions. Confused, anxious and worried, I couldn't go back to sleep, but I was afraid to let Bluebell know what I had just heard, so I decided to wait for a while and then pretend like I had just woken up.

I yawned, moved over and stretched softly. I saw Bluebell turning around to face me.

"What an early bird you are."

"I'm cold," I lied.

"Do you want me to close the window?" she asked as she was closer to it.

I nodded. I wasn't cold and I hated my bedroom window being closed but that was an issue for later.

"How come you're awake?" I asked as Bluebell was getting up to close the window.

"I have trouble sleeping in other people's houses."

Even in the night she would still wear those gloves, I realized, as my eyes fell on them.

"I see." It went silent for a while.

"Maybe we should go to your place soon," I proposed.

We had never been there before and she had never invited me.

She laughed it off. "My place is not nearly as nice as this. I don't really have people over."

"I would like to see it," I said, pushing her.

She shook her head. "Can't do, Junie."

I felt like it was a bad idea to keep pushing, considering how little I actually knew about her and all the suspicious activities that were surrounding her.

I still felt like she was my friend … but I also started to feel like I really had to start figuring some things out for my own good. She brought on a weird feeling in me. Being in her presence felt safe but as soon as she left, I started to feel panic, as if I were now in trouble. Something was drawing me to her, but she was a complete mystery, and she didn't even try to tell me about herself. She had only warned me and assured me she was looking out for me. And now had I accidentally heard her telling someone outside my bedroom window that she would give her life for someone, possibly me?

"I don't think I can go back to sleep," I said as I looked at my phone. It was only three in the morning.

She smiled faintly at me. "Wanna go for a walk?"

I froze for a second. *Walk? In the middle of the night? While there's a serial killer on the loose?*

"Don't worry about him," she said, while looking at me. I knew she meant Devlin.

Hesitantly I agreed and we got ready to go outside. When I opened the front door, I almost had a heart attack because of a random cat that was sitting in front of the door, and was loudly hissing. The cat didn't try to attack but just kept hissing as we tried to pass it. Bluebell gave me a look as if to say – 'just ignore it' so we did and started walking.

"I love taking walks at night," Bluebell said, as the moonlight highlighted her wintry white skin. The odd scars on her face were the same white as the skin that wasn't scarred.

With every step we took, I inevitably started going over everything that I was dying to know in my head, but I knew I couldn't mention what I had heard earlier that night.

"Are you ever going to tell me more about what on earth happened that night? The night I almost got murdered by your brother?"

"He's not my brother." She brushed it off, "but no, I can't tell you."

"You know everything about me," I thought out loud while thinking about the comment she had made about my nightmares. "You never tell me about yourself."

"I don't like talking about myself," she said nonchalantly.

"Why?"

She hesitated for a second. "I just don't think I'm that interesting. I feel like you have much more to tell."

I chuckled. "Well, where are you from?"

"Here."

I rolled my eyes. "Is that it?"

She nodded. "Yeah, I was born here, I- I'm still here, nothing special."

"How do you live?"

"Alone."

"Do you have any pets?"

She shook her head.

I frowned, thinking about more questions. "What do you do? Do you study, do you work?"

She nodded. "Nature."

"You study nature?"

For the first time in the whole conversation, she looked at me and smiled. "I love nature. The animals, the plants, the flowers ..."

"You got the name for it."

We both laughed.

"It's a home study," she added, before I could ask more questions. "So, what are your big plans for the future?"

"I don't know, honestly." I sighed, "I was trying to save up to move away but everything is kind of on hold until I get myself back together."

"Move away?" she asked. "Where to?"

"Parabellum," I answered. She raised an eyebrow.

Parabellum was a country not too far away from Aspera, but it had little in common with it. Aspera was bigger, full of grasslands and was overall ... nicer. Parabellum was a country that many people tried to stay away from as some were worried that it was haunted. It was a beautiful country but there often seemed to be some unexplainable things happening there, I figured there was some extremely advanced organized crime going on. It greatly interested me, and I was sure I could find a job there to make use of my knowledge of the subject.

"That is a five-hour flight away from here, isn't it?" she asked. I nodded.

"What about it makes you want to go there?"

"The fact that nobody else wants to," I said and grinned.

"They don't? What's wrong with it?"

Before we could continue our conversation, we were disrupted by a bat flying by, almost hitting me. I dodged it and cursed but then laughed it off. Bluebell seemed extraordinarily annoyed.

"What's wrong?" I asked her.

"Nothing," she said, looking in the direction the bat had flown in, still visibly irritated. "Come on."

We continued the walk, with me talking about my fascination with Parabellum to Bluebell, who apparently had never heard of the situation there. Eventually, we went home and back to bed to get a few more hours of sleep and the next day Bluebell went home to study, leaving me on my own again.

I spent most of the day looking out of my bedroom window, ruminating over what could've happened down there the night before, who Bluebell could've been talking to and what on earth it had all been about.

As odd and mysterious as she was, *there was nothing even remotely intimidating about Bluebell,* I thought. *Why did she seem to be involved in all these dangerous situations?*

She was a little shorter than me and she was considerably skinnier than me, which wasn't a surprise seeing how little she ate. She was the same age and if it weren't for how roughed up she looked and the gloves she always wore, she would look like the girl next door – not like a criminal.

She seemed to like regular things and was interested in the simple things in life. We seemed to be opposites in that way. When we hung out, she would gladly listen to me telling her about my mum's bizarre work stories, or about some outrageous theory I had heard of but she was just as easily excited about the weather or what kind of bird was flying by. She seemed to just want to enjoy life. She also seemed like she actually did, in contrast to what she had been telling the other woman outside my window the other night.

I sighed. It had been a long day. I was missing Bluebell. I had nothing to do, and my body was riddled with anxiety as usual. I was not looking forward to going to sleep that night. Both times she had slept over, I had slept surprisingly well, and it was frustrating me that now I had to sleep alone again, and would probably have another night of ruminating, anxiety and frustration. And I did.

I sighed as I once again rolled over and looked longingly at the empty mattress on the floor where Bluebell had slept. I was missing her so much that it felt like it hurt. I was wakened from a nightmare again, my chest was hurting, and my heart was beating way too fast. I groaned in frustration and went to turn around when I heard a sound coming from my window.

Without thinking, I looked over, hoping ... Instead I was met with two beady, small eyes on top of a long, scaly body with a broad hood. There was a snake making its way into my bedroom ... and it wasn't a small one. It slowly slithered inside, through the open window before it suddenly scooted back out through the window as if someone was pulling it and I heard it drop to the ground. Then I heard footsteps running away.

I rushed up to the window and looked outside but there was no sign of either a person or the snake. I quickly closed the window and went back to bed but I was wide awake and startled. I put my head in my hands and tried to do some deep breathing. It helped a little bit, but it was not going to fix the panic over whatever just happened. With my trembling, sweaty hand I reached out to my phone and dialled Bluebell's number. She didn't pick up. I felt tears coming and just lay down and cried softly, not knowing what to do, feeling desperate and unsafe; feeling like I had felt when I had contemplated jumping off the bridge.

The same feeling came rushing back over me and the thoughts started becoming overwhelming when my phone rang. She was calling back.

"Hey, it's late, why did you call? Is everything okay?"

"Can you come over?" I squeaked through my tears.

"Uhm ... Yeah, sure, I'll be there as soon as I can."

"Thank you."

"Do you want to stay on the phone or just talk when I get there?"

"When you get here," I said softly.

"Okay, be there in a bit then, bye."

She hung up and I decided to watch some cute videos to distract myself; still facing the window in case the snake came back. I was dying to smoke but under no circumstances would I open that window again or go outside. *Shit,* I thought to myself, *I have to open the door for Bluebell.*

I didn't know exactly how long it would take. She hadn't told me where she lived other than 'on the edge of town', so, after a few minutes of watching calming video's I double checked the window and went downstairs to the front door and went to stand outside to wait for her, trying to ignore my feelings of panic. Luckily, I barely had to stand there for a minute when I saw her walking down the street towards the house. She waved and I bashfully waved back.

We quickly went inside and up to my bedroom where she sat down on the mattress she had slept on the previous night, the sight of which gave me a sense of serenity.

"So …" she said as she looked at me. "What's wrong?"

"I keep having nightmares," I said, my eyes were still red from crying, "and I slept with the window open and there was a fucking snake."

"A snake?" she said as she raised her eyebrows.

I nodded. "A big one with a fat neck."

Bluebell couldn't help but grin. "You mean a hood?"

"Whatever," I laughed.

"Sounds like a cobra …" she concluded. "What on earth would a cobra be doing here?"

"I don't know, maybe it escaped or something."

"How did you get rid of it?"

"I didn't, it fell."

Bluebell raised her eyebrows again. "It fell?"

"It came through the window and then it fell back out. It looked like someone pulled it back."

"Someone pulled a cobra back after it climbed through your window?"

"I don't know, it went away," I said irritably, then I started to tear up, "but I'm so tired of not being able to sleep … I'm just so tired."

"Do you want a hug or something?" she asked awkwardly.

I nodded and she sat down on the bed next to me and embraced me. She felt cold but it felt great against my sweaty, restless self.

"I haven't slept well in months." I sniffed. "The only good nights were when you were here. I don't get it."

"Well, sometimes it just feels safer when there's someone else around," she said, although it didn't make a whole lot of sense to me since my parents were in the house too and I was never really alone. She let go of me, to my disappointment.

"That reminds me, I was wondering if I could ask you a favour."

"Like what?" It felt like a weird time to bring something like that up.

"I was wondering if I could crash here for a while," she said. I lit up from the inside but didn't want to show it.

She continued. "I can't stay at my own place right now."

"What happened?"

"Problem with the roof," she said, sounding mildly annoyed at the problem. "It's going to take a while to fix it but in the meantime, I literally don't have a roof over my head."

I grinned. "Of course. I should ask my parents, but I don't think it'll be a problem."

"Thank you," she said with a smile, then she moved her eyes towards the window. "I'm glad it's good timing."

I smiled too. "Yeah, I hope I'll be able to get some more sleep." The thought was relieving.

"Well, let's try. I'm tired too."

For the next few days, I felt better for the longest period in months. It was as if, when I was with Bluebell, my body calmed down, my mind calmed down and I could recharge myself from everything that had been happening inside me. I was eating better; I went on late night walks with Bluebell every single day, I was sleeping better … Everything seemed to go better. Of course, my parents had agreed to letting her stay with us, and they showered her with more food and invitations to all kinds of things than she could handle.

Eventually, what seemed inevitable for me lately, my good days came to an end.

I was with Bluebell on one of our late-night walks on a chilly September night when she suddenly stopped walking and slowly turned around.

"What's the matter?" I asked, confused.

She didn't answer, then after a moment I softly heard her cursing under her breath. She looked as if she was trying to come up with solutions to a problem I couldn't see. Eventually she seemed to give up and let out a frustrated sigh.

"Are you really doing this?"

I couldn't understand who she was talking to.

Then, out of the blue, Bluebell quickly turned around again. I turned with her, still confused, and let out a shriek when I noticed that there was a woman standing in front of us now. I had no idea where she had suddenly come from.

They looked each other in the eye for a few seconds, and then Bluebell sighed again and softly cursed. "Junie, this is Rosa. Rosa, Junie," she then said.

"Rosabella," the woman said as she reached out her hand for me to shake. I hesitantly did so. The woman had a firm stance, almost military, and wore her brown hair in a tight, sleek bun. She had a serious look on her round face as well.

"What brings you here?" Bluebell said half sceptical, half curious.

"If you can't beat 'em, join 'em," Rosabella answered.

"Hm-hm," Bluebell answered, apparently knowing what the woman was talking about. "Why the change?"

Rosabella looked away and seemed less harsh after hearing that question. She looked down at the ground.

"I made a promise and I intend to keep it. If that promise now includes this girl too then I'll do what I have to do."

"Do what?" I chimed in at last.

Bluebell and Rosabella gave each other a look but ignored my question.

"Let's go home," Bluebell said decidedly.

"Hold on," I protested. All this talk behind my back was starting to get on my nerves. "Could either of you please explain to me what on earth is going on?"

Rosabella seemed a little startled and Bluebell looked at me sympathetically. "I can't," she said with sincere pity. "Honestly."

"No, just no! What is this promise you two are talking about?! And yesterday, outside my window, I heard you talking to someone!" I directed the last part at Bluebell, then a realization struck me. "It was *you!*" I turned to Rosabella and started feeling angrier and angrier. "You told her someone was going to kill me! And she called you Willow!" I said, as I shifted my eyes between the two women. They both looked dumbstruck.

"Shit!" Rosabella cursed, her gathered demeanour now looking defeated, giving Bluebell a look of pure spite. Then she gathered herself, took a deep breath and went back to what I assumed was her normal composure. Bluebell looked like she had just seen a ghost.

"This is bad, Will–"

"Will you stop calling me that?!" Bluebell hissed. "Don't be like them."

"Right, I'm sorry. But this is bad."

"This is what I mean!" I spat. "Why does she call you Willow? And who is 'them'?"

"I told you already, I can't tell you much, Junie," Bluebell said. "You know I don't get along with my family, right? Willow is the name I had before I ran away."

"Okay," I said as I processed the new information. "Are there people coming to kill me?"

"No," said Rosabella firmly.

"Okay," I said again, feeling like that wasn't the whole truth. "But there were?"

"You remember Devlin? He is dangerous," Bluebell said.

"I understood that much," I snarled. "Is he …?" I wanted to ask about the murders that had happened in town, and the cemetery, but Bluebell gave me a look of warning. "But you said *them*," I followed up, "them implies more than just … him."

She gave me the same look again. "You already know way too much. Can you please let this go? And try and trust us?"

"I don't even know her!" I blurted out. "And I don't know *you* that well either!"

"Rosa saved my life more than once," Bluebell said. Rosabella nodded, looking a little proud.

"Why did you say that it was your fault?! What is your fault? Why am I going to die eventually?"

"Shit Junie, how much did you hear?!" Bluebell whined, starting to look more panicked. "Please, stop asking questions."

Both Bluebell and her friend seemed to start getting agitated.

"Junie, we don't know each other well but I've known Bluebell for a very long time," Rosabella said, in a forced calm voice. "She cares about you. I care about her, so that means I will look out for you too. This is not a great time for you, but it will get better. Can you trust me on that? We will be looking out for you."

Bluebell looked at me with pleading eyes.

"I'll do my best," I sighed reluctantly. It didn't seem like they were going to answer anything I wanted to ask. A small smile appeared on Bluebell's face.

"Thank you," she said. I wasn't sure which one of us she was saying thank you to; maybe both of us, but it sounded genuine.

"Go home," Rosabella said, warmly yet a little bit strict. "Get some sleep."

"Great idea. Do you still want me sleeping over, Junie?" Bluebell asked carefully.

"Yes," I said without hesitation, to my own surprise.

Rosabella stuck out her hand one more time to me. We shook hands, exchanged affirming smiles and Bluebell and I turned around to walk back to my parents' house.

I looked over my shoulder one more time but saw that Rosabella had already disappeared like the wind. All that was behind us was a bird that flew over us and away.

"I wish I could tell you more," Bluebell said. "I'm sorry."

"Maybe one day," I said vaguely, not sure what to answer, since I was wishing the same thing. We made our way back home and lay down on our beds. After we said goodnight, I cast one more look at Bluebell, who was staring at the ceiling once more, a glimpse of moonlight striking down upon her copper hair and simultaneously on the scars around her lips. I was wondering if I would ever find out what was behind that quiet demeanour, behind those scars, behind the stories, her family, her friend Rosabella. I wondered whether I would ever find out why everything had changed so drastically ever since I had locked eyes with her after the accident.

My thoughts faded into the quiet of the night as I fell into a deep, serene sleep, feeling grateful that despite everything, I was at least looking at a few nights of sleep without more terrorizing nightmares.

Chapter Nine

It was a regular Tuesday evening when my parents asked me to come and sit at the dinner table with them to discuss something. I was sitting on the couch with Bluebell when they asked, who remained on the couch when I got up.

"Actually, Bluebell, you should probably sit with us too," said my father.

She got up a little hesitant but joined us at the table.

"So, as you know we've been investigating a lot," started my mother, "but there hasn't really been any valuable information that could help us find out who did it."

She was talking about the murders that had taken place and the burial site that had been discovered. "Besides what you described to us, We took your description from the other night very seriously and the man you described is considered our number one suspect even though we have no idea who he is yet," she said, letting out a sigh after finishing the last part of the sentence, "but then your father came to me yesterday with something very interesting."

"Yes," he said, "I have been assigned a new client. Long story short, what he's been telling me is considered valuable information for the investigation your mother is working on, so he is working with the police now to hopefully help them figure this all out."

Bluebell and I looked at each other for a second, and then looked back at my father, waiting for him to continue.

"He's been describing a man to me who sounds just like the man you two encountered."

I felt my breath stop for a moment. Bluebell was looking dumfounded.

"Oh," was the only thing that managed to come out of my mouth.

"We were hoping that you two could meet up with him at the station so we can confirm it is the same man you are describing. It would help us a lot," my mother concluded.

I looked at Bluebell, not knowing what to say.

"Of course, we will come," she said and smiled, as if it wouldn't be a problem at all. "We'd love to help."

"Great," my mother said relieved. "I'll make the call right away."

She scheduled a meeting at the station for the next morning.

"So, I can't ask any questions, but the police can?" I asked while I was smoking in the window in my bedroom. I had started to smoke a lot less now that Bluebell was constantly around, but the thought of having to go to the station and talk about all this stuff with detectives had made me reconsider.

Bluebell was lying on her mattress, staring at the ceiling once more, but looking more distant than usual. "Not now, please," she said shortly.

I blew out the smoke and watched it fade into the night sky. Tomorrow was going to be a lot.

When Bluebell and I came downstairs the next morning, dressed to leave for the station, we found my father sitting at the table looking greatly stressed. There was a box with a bow on the table.

"Are you okay, Dad?" I asked, as we walked towards him.

He looked down at his coffee.

"Callista brought you some doughnuts." I went up to the doughnut box, saw a little note with a heart on it and couldn't help but smile a little. "The meeting is cancelled," my father mumbled, resting his head on one of his hands and staring about looking rather depressed.

My smile disappeared. "What do you mean? Where is Mum?"

He sighed and looked up, in his eyes a remorseful look. "My client is gone."

"Gone? The guy we were meeting up with?"

"Rune, yes," he said melancholy.

"Did he …?"

Bluebell was surprisingly quiet, still standing in the doorway we came through.

"He was murdered too," my father said. "He was left in front of my practice."

"Shit!" I cursed. "In front of the practice? What's the point of that?!"

"Sounds like he was trying to leave a message," Bluebell said suddenly. I looked at her and found her looking at me with a look that I could only interpret as her trying to get me to connect the dots.

"Yes," my father said, "your mother said they probably did this to make a point. That he shouldn't have talked."

"Poor guy just wanted to help," Bluebell said softly.

"He was a good man."

"I'm sure he was, Mr Lunis."

"The body – Was it …?" I asked.

My father nodded. "Same as all the others; with tons of bite marks. What kind of sadistic person would do all this?"

Bluebell remained silent. I just nodded at him, not really knowing how else to respond. I decided to go outside for another cigarette, processing all of this. Bluebell followed me.

"You knew this would happen, didn't you?" I asked softly.

She nodded hesitantly. "The only reason he is not coming back for you is because I am around, Junie. But we can't make this bigger than it is. It doesn't end well."

"So, you're just gonna let him keep on killing people?" I snarled, still silently, so my dad wouldn't hear.

"He's going to leave soon. I can't do anything," she said and looked at the ground.

"Leave to where? Isn't he just going to continue somewhere else?"

She remained silent. She tried to look up but squinted and looked back down when she saw the unusually bright sunlight.

"Let's just hope he's gone soon," she concluded, and she turned around and went back inside.

Chapter Ten

Vices

I didn't know if it had something to do with there being yet another murder in town, this time even one that hit closer to home, but tensions were running high all around me after that day. My mother was stressing over the case and everyone's safety. My father had difficulty working since the corpse of one of his patients had been placed right outside his practice – plus, he was upset with me to begin with, as he had just found out I had skipped several appointments with Donald and was now avoiding making a new one altogether – and Bluebell had been starting to act more and more restlessly. She was extremely easily agitated, had become distant and often left me wondering how long it was going to take until her house was fixed. Maybe the fact that one of her relatives was on a murder rampage was becoming too much for her. I was conflicted between keeping my mouth shut for my own, and apparently Bluebell's safety, and alternatively speaking up so possibly I could prevent any more people from getting hurt.

The fact that I didn't have any answers made it even more conflicting because I simply didn't have enough information to truly understand what was going on. Finally, my friends told me that they wanted to speak to me face to face about something, but we hadn't picked a time yet so that was a worry for another time.

"Do you maybe need some time to yourself?" I finally asked Bluebell, after she had snarled something under her breath at me for what must have been the tenth time that day.

"No."

"Maybe it'll do you good."

"I told you I can't do that."

"You could just take a walk or something, nothing is gonna happen in thirty minutes."

She snickered. "If you only knew."

"Maybe if you …"

She got up, sighed and paced around. "Maybe you're right. I'll be out tonight."

"Tonight?" I asked anxiously. "Why not during the day?"

"I have somewhere to be," she answered vaguely. "I'll ask Rosa to stay near you in case anything happens. You won't even notice she's around."

"What do you mean? She can come inside. That's not a problem."

"It's better if she doesn't," Bluebell said and looked at me. "Will you be okay?"

"Well, I won't be able to sleep." I sighed. "Maybe I'll stay up until you're back."

"I'll try to be quick, but it could be a while."

I shrugged. "Better than getting stuck in nightmares. Where are you going anyway?"

She gave me a look that implied she couldn't answer that so I let it go.

That night she left around midnight and assured me I would be safe with Rosabella around, wherever she might be. She told me to stay inside the house, keep the windows and doors closed and just entertain myself until she got back. I kept myself busy with silly TV-shows, still not being able to bring myself to watch my usual macabre shows, and the delicious garlic fried rice that Bluebell had insisted on making as a thank you for letting her stay over; but time never seemed to go by so slowly.

I felt beaten down, I was continuously trying to steer my mind away from suicidal thoughts and I was smoking a whole lot once again, even with the window closed.

The extreme shift in my mood after she left was worrisome. But I waited and waited and waited. Until two a.m., three a.m., four a.m., five a.m., six a.m., seven a.m., …

At just after eight a.m., when I was exhausted, frustrated, my throat was sore and I was angry that she hadn't come back yet,

I heard the doorbell ring. I was happy that my parents had both just left for work because I wasn't prepared for what I saw when I opened the door.

Rosabella was holding up Bluebell, looking worse than I had ever seen her. Rosabella didn't even greet me but immediately made for the stairs, dragging Bluebell upstairs and putting her on my bed. I followed them and closed and locked the door behind us when we were inside. Bluebell did not look amused by the whole debacle.

"What on earth happened to you?"

"I found her trying to hurt herself, so I brought her back here," Rosabella said.

"Hurt yourself? What on earth would you do that for?!"

Bluebell just stayed silent and looked disapproving. Her wavy red hair looked wild and quite honestly, she looked like she'd been hit by several trucks. She was bleeding from the mouth and there was also blood all over her clothes. She didn't seem to be in pain.

"Did you get attacked?" I asked concerned.

She just nodded.

Rosabella looked equally worried and frustrated. "Those clothes are not salvageable; do you have some spares that she can borrow?"

I nodded and went to my closet to get her a set of clothes. I offered them and Rosabella took them and shoved them in Bluebell's hands. "You need to shower. Thank you, Junie."

They went to the bathroom and I sat down on my bed and looked at a bloodstain next to me on my sheet. I was wondering what on earth she had gotten herself into. I was also feeling extremely worried. Had she been attacked by Devlin or another relative? Or by some animal? What could have happened? Rosabella quickly came back into my room, holding Bluebell's dirty clothes and instantly noticed the bloodstain on my sheet.

"Would you get up, please?"

I did. She grabbed hold of my blankets and pillow and held them. "I'll bring you new ones later." And with that, she walked out and after a moment I could hear the front door close behind her.

Left confused and dumbstruck, I didn't really know what else to do except wait for Bluebell to return. I lit a cigarette and started smoking out of my window. Before I could finish it, Bluebell returned wearing my clothes. Somehow, she had done a complete one eighty and almost looked as if nothing had happened. She sat down on my empty bed.

"Are you okay?"

"I'm fine," she mumbled, her expressions not particularly looking fine.

I took another drag from my cigarette. "Were you really attacked or did you get into a fight or something?"

"What's the difference?" I looked at her in disbelief. She rolled her eyes. "Let's stick with attacked."

I observed her, she looked better than she had in a while, even if she just had been fighting – even the scars on her face seemed to be less prominent.

"How come you look so … fine?"

"Never heard of make-up?" she asked nonchalantly.

"I didn't know you wore any," I answered, wondering where she could've got make-up in such a short time frame. I was fairly sure she didn't have any with her since she'd been here for a while.

"Sometimes it's necessary," she said as she shrugged.

I took a final drag and put out my cigarette. "Listen, Blue, I know you don't talk about yourself a lot but … I'm here for you if you ever change your mind."

Looking at her face, that somehow seemed to strike a nerve with her, but she recomposed herself before she spoke.

"Thank you."

Later that day, Rosabella came back as she had promised and brought me new pillows, blankets and sheets. She quickly made my bed for me and then asked if she could 'borrow' Bluebell for a bit. Secretly, I was reluctant, as I was aware of how I felt when she left, and also because I still wasn't feeling particularly safe, but Rosabella seemed to insist, insisting even harder after Bluebell had refused at first. Bluebell assured me that she would be back soon and that they would be close by in case anything happened; and of course I could always call her, she said. She went with Rosabella, while huffing and whining in the process, but eventually they left. Once again, I found myself smoking out of the window when I suddenly received a phone call from Bluebell, barely ten minutes after she had left. I answered the call. I heard no voices from the other side, just the sound of running. This went on for probably a few more minutes. It was probably a pocket dial, but I kept listening still.

Why would they be running? Was it even them, running so fast? It seemed unrealistic. Finally, the running stopped and I heard something that sounded like a very heavy door opening and closing. Then I heard some pacing. Finally, I heard a voice.

"This can't go on." It was unmistakably Rosabella.

"I lost control, I …" Bluebell said in a scared voice.

"That is the problem," Rosabella hissed. "You constantly surround yourself with these loathsome humans and then you're surprised when you lose control? You're better than this, Bluebell. You were covered in blood for crying out loud. You looked like a walking crime scene! And then you're out there looking like a fool hurting yourself with silver? Have you learned nothing?!"

"They're gonna catch me, aren't they?"

"No, they're not. This is all gonna be put on Devlin, no doubt about it."

"How do you know? They found the fucking bodies, Rosa. This has never happened before!"

"No one is gonna be able to prove it's you. Everyone suspects Devlin. The only trace that could lead people to you will be Junie. We just got to make sure that she doesn't talk."

"She won't," said Bluebell firmly, "but you're forgetting that Devlin killed that other guy. Now only Junie is alive to testify against him. She's next."

"Their whole investigation is already focused on him. You've just got to control yourself." That last part had an almost threatening tone to it. "If this continues, then sooner or later she'll stop trusting you and you could become a suspect. She will talk. And you know what that means."

There was silence for a moment. "Yes," Bluebell said softly.

"So, who was it?"

"I – I don't know," Bluebell stammered. "It happened before I could think straight. I was running through the woods when …"

"You were hunting in the woods?!" Rosabella said, once again almost hissing. "The woods that are now considered a crime scene?! You could've been seen!"

"Not those woods, I'm not stupid. Fuck. And that's not even what I mean. I needed a human. I had no choice."

"Right, so the woods wouldn't make a lot of sense …"

"No, it wouldn't. I only was running through Tumulo Forest because I wanted to stay away from here. Even if it was just for Junie's sake. So, I went to Insons. I … I found someone walking alone on the edge of town. He was middle aged, I think."

"So, what was wrong with him?"

"Nothing," Bluebell said, her voice breaking. "I lost it."

"Where did you take him?"

"All through Saecula." Her voice started to become softer and squeakier.

"You didn't bury him?"

"He wasn't very … intact anymore."

I snapped out of the trance I was in while listening to the conversation my cigarette had burned all the way up and burned my finger. I put the burned-up filter in the ashtray and sat down on my bed, shocked.

Did I just listen to a murder confession? A *multiple* murder confession?

Chapter Eleven

Ubel

After an estimated thirty minutes of sitting on my bed with my head in my hands in shock, I decided to run downstairs, lock the front door and turn off my phone so Bluebell couldn't reach me. Then I ran back upstairs, closed my window and started pacing around, thinking about what to do. I was sure the police could retrieve the phone call. They could listen to it and hear what I just heard, right? That ought to be enough proof in itself. I quickly grabbed my phone, turned it back on and was about to call my mother when I heard my window open and I froze in fear.

"You must be Junie," said a low voice.

"Who are you?" I asked, still facing the opposite direction.

"I am Ubel, of course. I believe you know my daughter."

I slowly turned around and laid my eyes on someone who looked worse than anything I ever saw in the state of sleep paralysis. Standing by my window was a tall, sturdy man with jet black hair and the same eerie, inexplicably white eyes that I had seen once before on Devlin. His skin was white, he was wearing a jet-black suit and holding sunglasses in his left hand.

"Willow," he added, "I believe you know Willow." I was still too shocked to answer, I felt frozen in place, like time was standing still. "No need to be so shy," he said in his deep voice and smirked. As he smiled and spoke, I could see he easily had the biggest canine teeth I had ever seen on a person. "I've heard a lot about you. Quite the special human you must be for Willow to keep you around for so long. I heard last night she snatched some fellow from Insons who was just taking a stroll … You must be testing her patience quite a bit."

"You – you're her father?"

"Ah, so she speaks," he smirked as he started to move around my room, looking at my belongings with fascination. "I am."

"Bluebell is my friend," I said and swallowed nervously.

"Bluebell? Still playing pretend, I see ..." he said. "Her name is Willow. And do you really want to be friends with a murderer? I hear you aren't fond of my son ... And that while he was so excited for you. The two of them are not so different, after all."

"W-what do you mean?"

"My son, Devlin. He told me Willow broke you two up the other night. Such a shame she felt the need to deprive her own brother of, well," he said while eyeing me up and down, "haven't you figured out by now what she really longs for?"

"Enough!" I heard from behind me as someone stormed through the door. "Get out, now."

"Ah, my weeping, weeping Willow. I was just talking to your little friend here."

"You have no reason to be here," she snarled. I found it very brave of her to speak like that to a man who, not even taking his eyes and teeth into consideration, looked like a beast.

"I was just asking her how well you two know each other. I imagine she must have a lot of questions after that conversation she just accidentally heard ..." he said and smiled widely. "Time is ticking, Willow. It would be a shame if you had to miss a feeding. We've all seen how you especially like those ... *inevitable* feedings."

"Stop it," she said, angrier than I'd ever seen her before. "That's not going to happen."

"My weeping Willow, as difficult as ever. You simply have no choice."

"Liar," she huffed.

"Time is ticking," Ubel said tauntingly, walking closer to me and reaching a thick finger out to caress my cheek. "I presume you won't be happy either if someone else cuts in line. Your brother is a tenacious one."

"He won't. She belongs to me."

"Oh, but does she really if your only intention is to ... keep her, as a mere pet? There will be a day when one of you loses control," Ubel said, removing his finger and walking to face Bluebell now. "This is only torture for both of you. History will repeat itself."

"It won't and she'll be okay. Not that it's any of your concern anyway."

"I am very concerned about my daughter and her appetite, just as I am with my son. I wouldn't want anything to stand in the way of a feast that is right under his nose."

Bluebell looked like she was about to jump out of her skin, Ubel's calm and collected tone did not help her mood. She took a moment to compose herself and then turned to me.

"What conversation is he talking about?"

"I, when you ..." I stuttered, struggling to form a sentence.

"Your little friend here was eavesdropping on you and that chameleon of yours," Ubel said, delighted.

I felt the blood drain from my face.

"I wasn't eavesdropping, I swear. It was a pocket dial."

"You sick son of a bitch," Bluebell said, and if looks could kill, Ubel would be triple dead now. "Why are you doing this? Don't you have anything better to do?"

"You're endangering our kind, Willow. You must make a choice. Feast, or gain yourself a mate, but don't fool yourself by thinking you can keep this charade up forever."

"I can't make that choice for her, and I won't," she hissed, taking a threatening step forward, despite her non-threatening ... well, everything.

"Time is ticking, Willow. If you don't hurry, someone might just swoop in and make the choice for you. I'll give your best wishes to Devlin and the others." He cast a last condescending look at Bluebell, gave me the same lustful, eerie look Devlin had given me on the night he almost attacked me, and then sped out of the room. Bluebell and I were silent until we heard the front door click as it closed.

"Shit!" was the first thing Bluebell said, as she was staring, looking panicked.

I was still taking everything in, not sure what had just happened.

She turned to me. "Junie ... What did you hear?"

"Enough to know that you should get out. I'm calling my mum as soon as you leave here."

"Please, don't do that."

I was not in the mood to argue with her. I heard what I heard, and I knew enough.

Bluebell started pacing around, stressed, trying to figure out a solution. She couldn't seem to find one.

"Would you just hear me out, please?" she pleaded eventually.

"No!" I said in an offended tone. "Get out! You're a criminal! If you don't leave, I'm going to call the cops!"

"Junie, please ... If I leave, you'll be in danger."

"If you leave, I'll be in danger?" I chuckled. "You yourself said you're a murderer! You *and* Rosabella, and you say she's protecting you? From what, the NCA? Get out, now!"

"Don't you think if I wanted to kill you, I would have done that by now!" Bluebell suddenly yelled. "I'm not joking, Junie, if I leave, they will come back. Devlin will come back, and he will kill you!"

"Why do all of you keep saying someone's going to murder me?! Why me?!"

"I can't tell you that," Bluebell said, moving her hands through her hair in frustration and despair. "I need you to believe me!"

"Why would I?"

"Okay," she sighed. "Don't you remember that guy that was seeing your dad? Rune? Remember what happened to him?"

"Yes, your *brother* killed him."

"Yes, he did. Do you understand why?"

"Because he was going to talk?"

"It's more than that," she said desperately. "I know about your nightmares. I know they started from the moment you woke up after the accident. I know they haven't stopped since and I know you are miserable without me now. I know you can't sleep without me; I knew that before you told me. I know everything. Rune was going through the same, except with Devlin. There's a reason why he was the only one who could say what he looks like

75

besides you. Once it starts, there's no going back from it. Therapy wouldn't have done a thing. Devlin set his mind on him, and he was dead immediately after that moment. It was inevitable. He was going to die, whether he talked to the police or not."

"But ... why? Why was he going to die? Why am I not dead?"

"Because I'm *protecting* you!" she yelled. "I don't want you to have that fate! I intervened when you met Devlin for that very reason. Otherwise, you'd be dead! I told you – the only reason he hasn't come back yet is because I'm here. I told him you belong to me. But they are getting impatient. They know I'm not going to kill you, that's not what I do."

"But it is! You said you killed someone! And that guy just implied you'll do it again!"

She sighed in frustration and put her hand to her forehead and squeezed her eyes shut. "That was different."

"What? How is that different? You–"

"We have to leave," she suddenly decided, looking as if she was making a plan in her head.

"Leave? *You* have to leave, I'm staying right here," I said stubbornly.

"Oh, for the love of ... I can keep you safe. But you have to come with me."

"Why can't I stay here?"

"Because you can't."

"Why?"

"Because they will let themselves in."

"And they won't do that at your place?"

"They respect my territory."

"*Territory?*"

"Yes. They are horrible but they do follow certain rules that exist among ... us."

Weird, I thought to myself. But there was no way on earth I was leaving with this murderer.

"Look," she said, "They know I won't kill you. Devlin will. He wants to, and Ubel will make sure he gets his way. If you stay here, with or without me, you'll be dead soon. It'll be slow, painful and torturous. I can save you, but you'll have to come with me."

"Tell me again why I can't just call the police? They'll keep me safe and throw all of you in jail."

"They won't stand a chance," she said without hesitation. I looked at her in disbelief. "Let me put it this way; you involve other people in this, and they die too."

I frowned, and then sighed deeply. "Hypothetically, where would we go?"

Chapter Twelve

Gotcha

Out of fear of being responsible for creating more victims, I had reluctantly agreed to go with Bluebell to wherever she lived and we started preparing, but first I figured I had to talk to my friends. They had already expressed their discontent about how often I was hanging out with Bluebell, and that since I had started seeing her, I quite literally had never tried to hang out with them again. I had never told them anything sketchy about everything that had been going on with her, and I was fairly sure that my mother was still giving them updates on me now and then, as they had never managed to speak a negative word about Bluebell as a person.

Knowing my mum, she was probably praising her to my friends for having saved me and being such a good friend to me, unfortunately at the cost of my old friends – although she had also been encouraging me to meet up with them as well.

It made me feel bad, I did really care about them, but I just felt … preoccupied. There wasn't anyone else I wanted to spend time with. I just wanted to be around Bluebell.

Deciding it was the right thing to do, I went over to their apartment to have the talk on the Tuesday night. It felt more like an intervention. Upon entering, the only one who happily greeted me was Dasch. My three friends were sitting on the couch, looking gloomy.

After a reluctant "Hi," I sat down on the empty couch and waited for them to start the conversation.

Davin started after casting a look at his sad looking girlfriend and friend.

"Junie, it's just … We've been trying so hard to keep up with you and we kept trying even though it seemed one sided. We tried to be understanding and we really thought things were getting better after Callista came to see you but … then we found out through your mum that you have been hanging out with other people, but not us."

"How come you didn't tell us?" asked Stellan, raising his blond eyebrows far above his glasses.

"I don't know," I answered. "I just didn't know what to say."

"Or is it because you knew you were pushing it?" asked Callista with a snarl.

"Who is this person anyway?" asked Davin. "Are you two dating or just hanging out?"

"We're just hanging out."

"So, you just went ahead and made a new friend instead of dealing with us? Is that how you deal with things?" asked Callista.

Davin looked at me with raised eyebrows, clearly feeling the same way. He was picking at his skin in frustration.

"Look," I said, "why is it so bad that I have another friend? Am I not allowed to?"

"Of course you are," said Stellan irritably. "The problem is that you just replaced us like we're nothing to you!"

"I've tried my best to stay in touch," I said. "It's just been hard, all right?"

"And you think it has been easy for us? We've done everything for you these past months!" said Davin.

"Well, I'm sorry," I said passive aggressively, "were you expecting to get a trophy for that or what?"

Davin looked like a fire had lighted in his eyes. Stellan looked down at the floor, defeated. Callista looked nothing but hurt. Dasch was lying at my feet, staring at me with huge puppy eyes.

"*Clearly* this was a mistake," I said. I gave Dasch a last pat and rushed towards the door.

I made my way out, let out a frustrated sigh and started making my way home.

When I arrived after what seemed like forever, I rushed inside and sped up to my room.

I noticed that the shower was on and rushed into my bedroom to have a minute to myself, but then I almost tripped over

Bluebell's bag. I bent over to lift the bag to put it to out of the way but almost pulled a muscle because it was a lot heavier than I expected.

"What the …?" I was resisting the urge to look inside out of respect (and perhaps fear as well) when I noticed something that was sticking out so much that it almost fell out. I couldn't help picking it up and realized it was a small device. I wasn't sure what it did, so I pushed a button and a flame came out. It was a small blowtorch. I raised my eyebrows, turned it back off and put it back. I couldn't help but look inside the bag after that. My eyes fell on a large, empty plastic bag that was hard to miss. There was no sticker on it or anything that would imply what it was used for, but it reminded me of one of those bags that are used in the hospital for liquids and transfusions.

I had a frown on my face but quickly snapped out of it when I heard some sounds coming from the hallway. I zipped up the bag and put it in the spot where she would normally leave it. I quickly sat down on my bed as if I had been there all along.

In walked Bluebell, smelling like sweet, flowery shower gel and the deodorant I let her borrow. It reminded me to put on some extra myself as I realized how unusually hot it was in my bedroom.

"How's the packing going?" she said as she put down her toiletry bag and put her worn clothes in a bag that was next to one I had just put back in its regular spot. She didn't seem to notice that it had been moved.

"Good, I'm almost finished."

"We have to leave before midnight," she told me. "No time to waste."

I nodded. We had told my parents we would be going on a trip together and weren't sure for how long yet, but luckily Bluebell managed to get plane tickets that we could show them. They were supportive and figured it would be good for me to take some time away after everything that had happened. We were all set to go now.

I started to get thirsty from the sudden warmth I was feeling.

"I know," I said as I looked around for my water bottle but couldn't find it. "Hey, do you want something to drink?"

"No thanks," she said and gave me a small smile.

I nodded and went downstairs, figuring I must have left the bottle there.

I made my way to the kitchen and couldn't help but notice a book on the kitchen table. My father was always a big reader, so I figured it was his and I decided to check it out. It was a book called *Bloodthirst* and on the cover were a set of teeth with gigantic fangs for canines, dripping with blood. It made me frown, thinking about how, if vampires were actually real, one could surely think they'd have something to do with the case. I shrugged it off.

I grabbed my bottle and went back upstairs. I didn't make it much further than the top of the stairs, however, because when I started walking towards my bedroom, I stepped on something sharp and let out a shriek. I looked at my foot and noticed there was a nail that I had stepped on. It had punctured my skin. I hissed while I pulled it out and noticed that I was bleeding a bit.

"Everything okay out there?" Bluebell asked from my bedroom.

"Yeah, I'm fine, just stepped in something."

I walked up to the bathroom, threw the nail away and turned to sanitizing the small wound and put a band aid on it.

"I'm going to get some fresh air for a minute, okay? I'll be right back," said Bluebell.

"Sure," I said, as I walked back into my room, expecting her to walk past me towards the front door, like any normal person would do, but I noticed my window was open and Bluebell was gone.

"Of course," I sighed. *Of course she wouldn't take the door like normal fucking person.*

Still hot, I walked over to the thermostat, and I noticed that the temperature was way up from what I normally had it set at, so I turned it back down and took a few sips from my water bottle. I continued packing.

After about thirty minutes I started wondering where Bluebell was and started feeling increasingly uneasy.

"Blue?!" I yelled from out of my window. No response. I looked on my clock and decided I would go outside to look for her if she hadn't returned in fifteen minutes. She didn't.

I closed my window and made my way outside. I walked around the house but saw no sign of Bluebell. My anxiety started to increase, and I wasn't sure what to do. I wanted to go look for her, but I also felt scared to go out on my own.

I decided to call her – the call was answered right away.

"Blue! Hey, I was wondering if everything was okay? Where are you?"

"Helloooooooo," said a voice that was unfortunately familiar to me.

"Hello? You're no fun," complained Devlin on the other side of the line. "Willow is with us, we're having a little family reunion."

"W-why? Did you take her?"

"Let's say she wasn't *ecstatic* to see us waiting outside when she inevitably flew out of that window of yours," he said in a taunting tone, "but we managed to convince her to come with us."

"You didn't convince her, you forced her," I snarled.

"Potato, potaato."

"Where is she?"

"Are you aware that there is an abandoned property only a few miles away from you?"

"Abandoned? No, I don't know what you're talking about …"

He sighed. "Explosion, the tragic loss of life of some … cooks."

"The old drug lab? By the hospital?"

"Yes," he said impatiently.

"I'll be there as soon as I can."

"Bye, bye then," he said teasingly and hung up.

Shit, I thought to myself. I stood still for a moment then turned around to run inside.

"Junie!" I heard from behind me and saw Rosabella running up to me, she was bleeding and looked as if she had been attacked by some animal. "They took Bluebell."

"I know," I said in a more miserable voice than I had intended.

"You know?" she asked, surprised. "Let's go inside."

We quickly made our way up to my bedroom – not that there was anybody home, but just to be sure.

"What happened to you?" I said as I took a good look at Rosabella. She was normally so polished, so *together*, she always looked to me like a mother who was on her way to take her children to the best school in the country. Strict and with a no-nonsense attitude towards everyone, but with the best intentions. Now, however, she looked more like a mother who had just tried to protect her children from a bear attack.

"I, uhm, tried to fight them. Needless to say, it didn't go that well. They got away."

"What can I do? What do you need?"

"Nothing, just some time," she said dryly, "but thank you."

"Are you sure? You ..."

"I'm sure."

I smiled faintly. "We have to go there."

She laughed. "I am going to go there. You should stay here."

I frowned. "Excuse me? I'm not just going to sit here and do nothing when Bluebell is there being ... Who knows what they'll do to her!"

Rosabella sat down. "Has it occurred to you that it might be a trap?"

"A trap? For what?" Then it started sinking in. "Oh. He wants *me*."

She nodded. "And he is not alone. You can't go there. You won't last a second."

"But you can't fight them! We have to do something!"

"And we will. There's only one way and it's still risky."

"What way is that?"

She hesitated for a second. "You can't tell anyone about this, understood?"

"Sure," I said, feeling as if it didn't matter anymore because there was so much I couldn't talk about already. One more secret wouldn't change anything.

"Give me the clothes," she said, as she pointed at a pair of pyjamas that were on the floor next to me. I resisted the urge to tell her that I really needed to wash those and handed them to her. "It's best if you don't look."

"Okay …" I said, not knowing what on earth was going on. "I'll wait outside then."

I walked into the hallway, closed the door behind me and waited. I sighed, anxiously but I was also fed up with all the secrecy and the weirdness. I just wanted things to go back to normal, when my biggest problem was getting up on time to get to work.

"You can come back," Rosabella called from my room, "but be prepared, you're going to freak out."

Freak out? After seeing Bluebell's dead-eyed family I didn't think anything else would freak me out anytime soon; but of course, that thought went away as soon as I stepped back into my room and laid eyes on … me. Standing in my room was someone who looked exactly like me. She had the same face, the same body and the same hair and she was wearing my pyjamas. I didn't know what to do. I did, at that moment, suddenly understand why people said I looked like my parents as often as they did.

"Don't worry, it's me," my lookalike said, in my exact voice, "Rosabella."

"No," is the only thing I managed to say, "No."

"Sit down," the fake me said and gestured to my bed. I obeyed and sat down, tensed up. "There is a lot you don't know, Junie, but for now, you just have to understand that this is real, and that this is me. I am going to go over there and try and get Bluebell out safely."

"But how … You … You look like me."

"Yes, and if I come back, I will do my best to explain to you how I did it."

That snapped me out of it. "*If* you come back? You can't …"

"They are out to kill you. I look like you and hopefully smell like you enough for them to believe all it for just a moment.

If they believe it, they will kill me and if they don't, they will kill me too. Either way they will do it because of what I did."

"No," I said, panicking, "I can't let you do that, no!"

"I insist," she said calmly. "I need to try to get her out."

"Won't they just let her go if I don't show up?"

"Nothing would stop you from going over there to try and help and I think you know that. This is the only thing I can do to try to protect you both."

I swallowed my nerves. She was right. Bluebell was only gone for a bit, and I already felt like I was withdrawing. I would absolutely go over there, no matter what. I didn't get it, but at that point I knew that Rosabella did and seemed to continuously be ten steps ahead of me.

"I have to go, please stay put. Keep the doors and windows closed and locked. Is there still some of that garlic rice in the freezer that Bluebell made a while back? Maybe you should eat some of that." She sighed and got up. "If I don't see you again, I wish the best for you. My advice would be to listen to and trust in Bluebell. She is not like her family, and she's clearly got your best interest at heart."

She cast a last look at me and then walked out.

I heard the front door click and lay down on my bed, taking a minute to let it all sink in before going and locking everything up. I was panicked for less than ten minutes, when my phone rang. Incoming call from Bluebell. I anxiously picked up.

"Hello?"

"I don't like to be fooled," said Devlin, sounding a lot less playful than before.

I stayed silent. They figured it out. Was Rosabella dead?

"I suggest you make your way quickly or we might have to consider another way to settle this."

"Like what?" I asked with a lump in my throat.

"Hm, let's see ..." he said, "perhaps, if you're too cowardly to face us yourself, you could send in someone else. How about your mother? She seems lovely."

"Stop it."

"The choice is yours," he almost sang. "Be there within the hour."

"He's lying!" yelled Bluebell in the background. My breath stopped.

Then I heard a deafening screech.

"Our Willow is getting a little rambunctious ... Do you really want her to suffer in your place?"

"Shut up!" I snarled, trying to think but fighting back tears.

"Oh," he said amused, "I guess you are too."

"I'll be there," I concluded. "Just ... Don't hurt her."

"Time will tell." He hung up the phone.

"Fuck!" I whispered to myself, in tears now, while I put down my phone. But I had no time to cry. I grabbed my bag, went downstairs and grabbed a kitchen knife which I put into it. Then I remembered Bluebell's blowtorch and ran back upstairs. I pulled her bag near me, opened it and grabbed the blowtorch. I quickly searched for anything else that could be useful.

There was the empty bag I saw before, some extra gloves (what was the deal with these things?) and ... some sort of multi tool? It looked like a drill except the head was round. It looked like something you would work on a house with. Weird. I figured it might be useful and put it in my bag. The only other items were chewing gum, face wipes and a pair of blue contacts.

The last item made my heart skip a beat, as I was instantly reminded of Devlin and Ubel's terrifying, dead eyes without any colour in them. I silently hoped that she just did not like her eye colour or something and chose to wear blue contacts for the aesthetic and not because she looked like a monster without them. I put it aside in my mind as that was a problem for another time, and went back downstairs with the multi tool, blowtorch and kitchen knife in my bag.

I rushed out of the door and started making my way towards the former drug lab, running quicker than I had ever run before, trying to dodge the judging faces of citizens not waiting for someone to barge through the streets. I had no concept of time while I was running, only haste.

When the property was in sight, I started to feel my chest tighten – not just from the running – and a knot forming in my stomach. I couldn't ignore it anymore at that point. I looked to see if there was anybody around, took a deep breath and entered through the doorway – the door had been removed long ago. I stopped, once inside, to take the knife out of my bag and put it up my sleeve so I was at least a little bit prepared.

"Junie!" I heard from my left. "So glad you could make it!" It was Devlin's insufferable voice. I braced myself for what was about to come and followed the direction of his voice.

"Right over here, love," he said.

I walked into what I assumed was once a living room and was met by a widely smiling Devlin. His canines were longer than on my first encounter with him but other than that, little had changed.

For what had seemed like a thoroughly planned out encounter, the crime scene didn't look as elaborate as I would've expected. It was a mostly empty room, inside what was once a house – now merely a frame with a collapsing roof and burned furniture everywhere. The walls were mostly black in this room. You could see some white on certain walls and it was clear near which walls the massive explosion had taken place.

Devlin was standing in the back of the room and behind him was a chair. Behind the chair stood Ubel. He had his hand placed firmly on the shoulder of someone sitting on the chair, like a warning.

This someone was Bluebell. But she didn't look like the Bluebell I was with before. She wasn't wearing her signature gloves, and from where I was standing I couldn't see anything on her hands that would explain why she wore them so unchangingly, but it was odd to see her without them.

Her eyes weren't bright and blue anymore. They were just as dead as her family's. White as snow.

"I'm so sorry," she said remorsefully as if she had just committed a crime by letting me see her like this.

"Silence!" said Ubel's deep voice firmly, pushing his fingers into her shoulder. She flinched in pain.

Devlin started pacing around slowly, just like Ubel had done when he invited himself into my bedroom, still smiling at me.

"Now do you see what she really is?" he said, sounding like this was the best day of his life. "She's not your friend. She's not the hero she claims to be. Look at her, she's a monster!"

I felt bad for thinking it at that moment but ... she did look like a monster. She looked inhuman.

She wasn't restrained on the chair but she looked broken. She looked as if she was tired of trying and had given up on trying to get away.

"Not enough proof for you?" he said in response to my silence. "Father, why don't you show our guest?"

"Please ..." Bluebell pleaded, but it didn't matter.

Ubel pulled Bluebell, who looked even tinier next to him, up to her feet and took out a huge, shining silver half-moon blade and held it against her stomach. Before I could say anything to protest he slid it across her skin, Bluebell standing still but screeching like I had never heard from any person before, a look of pure agony on her face.

When Ubel took the blade off her she collapsed onto her knees, whimpering, silently begging for mercy. The gash was enormous but ... just white. Like ripped paper, it was niveous flesh, not that of a person who had just been cut open and should be gushing blood and entrails ...

"Now we wait a moment ..." said Devlin excitedly, tauntingly.

After a few seconds something started coming out of the wound, but it wasn't what I was expecting. It was a dark, thick substance that looked like slime. It came out as if in slow motion. And there were lumps. It was a deep dark red, with a few ... layers, almost, of black. It was a disturbing sight.

"That must be a shocking sight to see," Devlin said while keeping his eyes on me.

It was. It absolutely was. But I had to stand my ground.

"Let her go," I said. It didn't sound as assertive as I had hoped. It made Devlin and Ubel chuckle.

"Why don't we make a trade?" he suggested. "You surrender and your little friend here gets to roam free."

"Junie …" Bluebell whimpered, but before she could say anything else Ubel's hand was back on her shoulder, pushing into her skin, and she squeezed her eyes shut in pain. The thick fluid was still leaking from her stomach.

"Okay. I'll do it," I said, terrified, but I knew I would never be able to forgive myself for just standing by and doing nothing while someone, who besides everything had been nothing but kind to me, was being tortured.

"Great," Devlin said, "come here then."

I started walking over slowly, holding on to the knife up my sleeve, ready to pull it out and attack.

Bluebell's eyes were focused on me, her expression remorseful.

As I came closer she started trying to get out of Ubel's grip but even his one hand seemed to be enough to keep her in place. Eventually, he put his other hand around her throat and started pushing there too. Her screams were heart-breaking. It was enough for me to take the chance to use my knife.

I pulled it out, ran the last bit towards Devlin and with all the courage in my body struck the knife at him. To my surprise, he didn't try to stop me from stabbing him at all. He just stood there.

For a split second I thought I had done some damage, only to realize that he had a smirk on his face and the kitchen knife had simply bent on his chest.

I remained silent as fear took me. I surely didn't stand a chance now.

He pouted. "The poor human, her first proper interaction with a vampire and it'll be her last."

I heard Ubel chuckle through Bluebell's screams.

The word vampire got through to me, and in response I started to walk backwards. Devlin seemed to have had enough of waiting and his face turned serious.

Just as he lunged at me, long fangs fully exposed, I heard a loud shriek and something jumped in front of me and pushed me backwards with such force that I literally flew for a few seconds before I hit the floor.

I recognized Bluebell from behind. I looked over at the chair she had been sitting on and I saw Ubel on the floor, bleeding the same, thick substance that had been leaking from Bluebell, and the blade sticking out of his stomach.

I looked over and I saw Bluebell fighting off Devlin. They were throwing each other, biting each other, punching each other with force I had never seen before.

I tried to get to my feet but I flinched and fell back down. I looked at my leg and noticed that it was bent in an unnatural position; and at that moment I felt the pain. I had broken something. Defeated, I looked back to the source of the fighting uproar; Bluebell and Devlin were practically flying, throwing each other onto furniture and into the walls and digging their teeth into each other.

Bluebell's teeth weren't nearly as long as Devlin's but either way, her bites seemed to inflict a lot of pain onto him. I noticed Ubel was slowly starting to get up, rage all over his square face.

"Hey, over here," I suddenly heard from behind me, I looked up and saw Rosabella, looking like herself again. She didn't look good. She looked rough and she was sweating heavily. Her (my) clothes were covered in blood, and I noticed deep bite marks on her skin, still bleeding too.

"Rosa," I smiled faintly, relieved to see her. "You made it."

"Barely," she said as she knelt next to me, her face flinching, and examined my leg. Both of us looked up when we heard a loud scream and saw that Devlin was pulling the blade out of Bluebell. He had stabbed her, in her already open wound.

"She's not gonna make it," I said softly.

"Don't underestimate her," Rosabella said, eyeing Ubel, who was limping way to the back of the house, looking as if he was trying to run away. "I'm going to create a window and then you and I are out of here, understood?"

I nodded. It wasn't like I had plans to go off on my own now that I couldn't walk.

Rosabella ran towards Devlin, who had just been thrown onto the floor. Rosabella snatched the blade from where it had fallen and stabbed him with it, it went in deep enough to where I wondered if she had just nailed him to the floor with it. She got out of the way just in time because Bluebell flew onto him and started, well, beating him. I saw a rage in her that I didn't know she had. I quickly looked around the room and noticed that Ubel had disappeared.

Rosabella came running towards me now, then past me and away. I panicked for a second and then, much to my surprise, a being I had never seen before ran in, through where Rosabella had just disappeared. It looked like a tall, graceful white horse, except that it had ... wings.

Zoning out from everything else going on in the room, I stared at it as my jaw dropped open. It neighed as if it was trying to tell me something. I snapped out of my staring disbelief when I heard Bluebell scream.

"Go, Junie!" then she was thrown into a wall which I could've sworn cracked a bit. "It's Rosa!"

Right, I thought to myself. *I shouldn't be surprised.*

The majestic horse knelt in front of me. I could clearly see the cuts and bite marks on its velvety skin. I pushed myself up with my hands and leaned on my one good leg. I stumbled to the winged creature and climbed on it with my eyes screwed shut from the pain. It got back up, lifting me in the air and before I could properly get hold of its mane to brace myself, it started running.

I cursed out loud and quickly grabbed the thick, silvery hair.

It ran out of the backdoor, where the grasslands were, and pushed itself up into the sky. Holding on for my life, trembling with fear, we reached higher and higher altitudes, until the ground beneath us disappeared and all I could see was the dark night sky.

Chapter Thirteen

Home Sweet Home

I opened my eyes and could barely make out anything. All I saw was darkness. I gasped and quickly started looking around, to no avail. Where on earth was I?

"Relax, Junie, it's all good," I heard Rosabella's voice say from somewhere I couldn't make out. "Hold on."

I heard some shuffling and struggling and then some sort of light went on. I saw Rosabella standing across from me, cleaned up at last and in her own clothes but with wounds still visible.

"Ah, much better," she said contentedly while looking around the room proudly.

"Where are we?" I asked as I pulled myself up, flinching from the pain in my leg.

"This is where Bluebell lives."

"This is a house?"

I looked around the room, still struggling to see as the light didn't cover a lot of it, and I could only make out the hard, cold, metallic floor I was sitting on and some stuff lying around. It didn't look like a house.

"I guess you could call it that," she chuckled. "Here."

She handed me a flashlight. I turned it on and shone it around. Everything looked metallic, the floor, the walls, but it was extremely rusty. The room looked slightly orangey because of it. There were no doors or windows. I instinctively shone the light up to the ceiling and noticed a latch.

"Is this some kind of … bunker? Are we underground?"

She nodded.

"Where?"

"Saecula Forest. Have you heard of it? It's not too far from town. No one knows it's here."

I shone the flashlight around some more and analysed the bunker. It was just one small room. There was no furniture whatsoever; and no lights, other than the flashlight I was holding and the portable light that Rosabella had turned on. Not too far away from me I saw some more contacts lying on the floor, new in their packaging and there were also some contact containers, contact liquids, gloves, both new and some ripped and dirty. Beside them, I saw some clothes lying around, some of which looked just as old as the bunker itself. I shone the torch to my right and saw some tools lying around near the corner, even something that looked like an electrical saw. There were some bags there, most of which I recognized as being from the store I had been stalking Bluebell at when this all started. Next to them I saw a pile of … knives or daggers and bleach and cleaning aids.

It seemed as if she kept all her stuff just shoved into different piles scattered around the room. Besides the pile of clothes and contacts, the area was full of tools, bags and knives and there was one other gathering spot which consisted of books, magazines, dried up flowers and plants. When I shone my flashlight at Rosabella, I noticed she was standing near some sort of small skeleton. I cursed under my breath, and Rosabella just chuckled.

"I guess it's all on the table now, isn't it?"

I just nodded in disbelief. I felt sick to my stomach — it felt like I shouldn't be in this place at all. It felt sinister.

"Care for a snack?" Rosabella asked as she reached for a random bag. "You must be starving."

"I, uhm, I would rather not," I said, eyeing the pile of bones again.

"Ah," she said, understanding, putting the bag back down, "but still, you must be hungry, aren't you?"

"How long was I out for?" I asked with a frown. The last thing I remembered was soaring on the back of a winged horse. I didn't remember landing.

"Not that long, maybe an hour tops. But it's been quite a day. I wrapped your leg for you. It seemed … not right."

I looked at it. There were some sticks on the sides, bound together with rope.

"Best I could do," she said humbly.

"Thank you," I said as I chuckled. It seemed like nothing compared to the severity of the rest of the situation. "Where is Blue?"

"I hope she is hunting and regaining her strength," she said as her tired expression changed to a worried frown. She didn't need to say any more for me to understand. If she wasn't hunting, she was dead.

"Can vampires die? I mean, hypothetically," I said, still not wanting to give in to the ludicrous idea of vampires actually being real, as Devlin had claimed.

"Hypothetically," she said, smiling at my words, "yes, but not like you and me. Vampires can only die if they are killed by another vampire."

"Wow," I said as I finally put down the flashlight and just stared at the rusty, cold ground. "Speaking of you, what are *you*? You know, like, hypothetically."

Rosabella seemed to be enjoying these questions. "I am, in layman's terms, a shapeshifter."

"How does that work?"

"I can transform into other living beings, humans, animals ..."

"Flying horses."

"Pegasi," she said while looking at me in the faint light.

"Of course," I said sarcastically. "So they are real too?"

"Hypothetically, yes."

I looked at her and saw her smirk. I couldn't help but laugh a little.

"What about snakes?" I asked suspiciously, suddenly reminded of that very odd time a massive cobra slithered into my room.

Her smirk disappeared. "I owe you an apology for that, yes. I hope you can ... empathize with the fact that I was looking out for Bluebell."

"It's fine," I said as I literally waved it off. It wasn't fine, but it just seemed like the least of my problems at the moment. "So you're telling me that all these mythical beings really exist?"

"It's not fine. I truly apologize," she said. "But yes, they exist. If you're still sceptical I guess I could show you how I transform, if you want."

"That would help."

She stood in front of me, I picked the flashlight back up and shone it at her.

"Great," she said and grinned in response to the bright light directed at her. "Okay then."

She closed her eyes and it looked as if her body got effortlessly sucked up into a tiny black ball of darkness. There was nothing for a moment. Then another little black ball appeared, got bigger and a cute, fluffy little dog appeared. The little dog disappeared, shrinking back into the dark dot, only to return as an elegant swan. This went on for a bit and the animals got bigger. I saw a vulture, a regular horse, a giraffe that almost broke its neck because it was too tall for the bunker, a walrus, and a couple of different humans before she turned back to the soft brown skinned, polished Rosabella and wiping the sweat off her forehead she laughed.

"Convinced?"

"I guess I have no choice," I answered as she sat down next to me. She grabbed a snack out of the bag she had offered me food from and started eating, offering me again, but I couldn't let myself. It was as if the bones in the corner were looking at me. Through the crunches of Rosabella's chewing, I suddenly heard something from above and looked up to see the heavy, rusted latch opening. I instinctively held my breath with fear. In came Bluebell. She dropped through the hole and the heavy latch fell closed behind her. It was at that moment I realized that this is where they must have been when I overheard their conversation over the phone. She sat down against the wall to the left of us and let out a long, long sigh. Rosabella and I both looked at her, anxiously waiting for her to say something, happy that she was back but unsure of what was about to come next. She had bite marks and cuts all over but the huge cut on her stomach that was inflicted by Ubel seemed to have … healed. It was closed. She still wasn't wearing her gloves or contacts and her clothes were ripped and falling apart.

"He's going to come back," she finally said. "He is going to wait to ambush us."

Rosabella nodded. "And Ubel?"

"He's not going to risk getting hurt because of his minion. He might help to set it up the ambush for fun." She sighed, "but he won't fight. You saw him walk away."

Rosabella nodded again in understanding. "I'll keep watch."

I don't know how she did it, but Bluebell basically jumped up towards the latch and held it open. There weren't any stairs that could be used to climb up to or down from it. I was too focused on Bluebell to notice that Rosabella had gone, only realizing it when I saw a tiny little bird flying past Bluebell into the air outside the bunker. Bluebell dropped back down and sat back against the same wall. At that moment she must've realized that she looked like, well, a vampire.

"I'm so sorry," she said as she sprang up and started looking through her stuff. She ripped open a pack of new contacts and stuck them in her eyes, not being careful at all.

"No, don't − don't apologize," I said although I felt relieved when she had some colour back in her eyes. She sighed again and slid down against the wall once more.

"I wish you didn't have to see me like this," she said.

"Do you always wear those contacts?" I asked curiously. She nodded. "Look, Blue … I know you don't like to talk a lot, but I feel at this point that you do owe me some answers," I said dryly.

Of course, I was due some answers, I thought to myself. *I was almost murdered.*

"There's not much to hide anymore, I guess," she admitted. "Ask away."

She looked defeated and cornered. I was trying to figure out where to start.

"Why do you live here?"

She started laughing. "*That's* your first question? Well, I've lived here for a long time. It's comfortable for me."

"What is all of this stuff?" I asked, shining my flashlight over the items on the ground.

"Tools, gloves," she summed up dryly, "magazines."

"Yeah, what is it with those gloves? I never see you without them," I said, almost offended, then I realized she wasn't wearing them at this exact moment. "Except now, I guess."

She stuck out her hand, her palm on top. I wasn't sure what I had to look at.

"Look at the tips."

And so I did. I turned the light to her fingertips and leaned in to look. There were no fingerprints. Just faint ... scars.

"I burned them off."

I raised my eyebrows. "That sounds ... excruciating."

I decided to continue asking questions. "What are those ... tools? And why do you have blowtorches?"

I was fully aware that there were more important questions but it was nice to talk about stuff that seemed less serious than our lives being in danger at the moment.

She looked at me and opened her mouth to fully reveal her canine teeth that were longer than a few hours ago.

"I have to file them."

"Have to or choose to? Devlin and Ubel don't seem to care."

"Have to if I don't want to look like a monster," she said in a spiteful tone.

She hesitated for a second, as if she didn't want to admit to what she was going to say next.

She continued. "And I, uhm, I burn my nose."

"You what? Why? How?"

"Like this," she said and fetched a blowtorch, putting the opening at the bottom of her nostril.

"No, please don't."

She put it back down. "I'm not going do it now, you asked."

"And why?" I repeated.

"Why what?" she said as she sat back down. "Why do I shoot fire up my nose?"

"Well ... yes."

It started to dawn on me that all those scars she had … she must have inflicted them all herself. The scars on her lips, her nose … Even her burned finger tips that she always hid under her gloves. It was her own doing. Devlin and Ubel had set out to show me what she looked like when she wasn't doing all of that, what she *really* looked like, to the point of slashing her skin open, just to prove a point.

"I … I don't want to say," she said as she looked down.

"Okay, why do you burn your fingertips then? What's the point?"

She got up and started nervously walking around, looking majorly triggered.

"I don't want these fangs. I don't want these eyes. I don't want to have this sense of smell that makes it impossible for me live in this world because …" She apparently decided not to finish that sentence. "I have to burn my fingers, so I don't leave evidence when I …"

"When you kill someone," I finished.

She looked at me, a look of pain on her face. "I can't even cry, Junie. I physically can't." She leaned back against the wall and composed herself.

"I don't want to live like this." She finally concluded, "I don't want to take any more lives."

"How many have you taken?"

"I don't know," she said, shaking her head. "I honestly don't know."

"That cemetery …"

"Yes, that is mine. Everyone who lies there, I killed."

"But there were hundreds …"

"And there will be hundreds more," she said, as if it was written in stone. "I … I try to only kill when they are already dying."

I connected the dots. "Is that why you killed that lady and that kid?"

She nodded. "They were dying," she said, her voice breaking, but still no tears. "It's better than taking a life that is still … a life."

She started gazing as if she zoned out, "but even that is inevitable."

"You mean that night when Rosabella brought you in."

"I couldn't control myself anymore," she said, angry at herself. "They were right. This is not sustainable. I can't just be hanging around a human twenty four seven and expect that it'll all be fine. So stupid. So fucking stupid."

"So …" I said and swallowed nervously, "why is that?"

She looked at me as if I asked an incredibly stupid question. I stared at her, not speaking, just waiting.

"Because I have to eat," she eventually answered, looking away, "and you're not supposed to play with your food."

"I wouldn't call it playing."

She laughed, maniacally.

"Junie, do you know why it is that you react to me the way that you do? Do you get it?"

"No," I admitted.

"That night you were in that car crash, I came up to you to eat. I thought you were dying," she said as she started walking around again, speaking loudly, "but then you suddenly woke up, so I called emergencies and you recovered. Unfortunately, it's just not that easy."

"What do you mean?"

She sighed in frustration.

"When a vampire decides on a prey, they get it. *You* were supposed to be my prey that night. When a human encounters a vampire like that, it's like a curse. They are going to die. Everything in their body will bring them back to the vampire, one way or another. The prey starts getting self-destructive or they go through great lengths to get close to the hunter. Or both. It's not some unexplainable … state of mind. It's not a mental illness. It's not treatable. You're dead the moment one of us decides."

The way she said 'one of us' gave me the chills.

"Is that why you said that I … belonged to you, that night with Devlin?" I asked carefully.

"Yes," she said, sounding disgusted with herself. "The only way to get you out of that situation was to stick to that. If I had just left it like it was, you would've been dead, or you would be cursed by him now, and he wouldn't even think of sparing you."

"Why *are* you sparing me? You're torturing yourself to be around me. You killed someone else because of me. How is that better?"

She ignored my first question. "I shouldn't have killed him. I shouldn't have. I didn't want to, I just ... lost it. I can't let you die, Junie. I can't let this happen again. I'm the one who should die," she said in a desperate tone, "but I can't. I've tried ... for decades. I tried it again that night but it just won't work. I don't want you to die. I don't want anyone to die. I don't want to kill anyone. I wish I could just eat ... your kind of food. Pasta. Potatoes. All that stupid, easy stuff. I don't want to live like this."

I sat there in silence. "That sounds really hard," was all I could manage to say.

"Yeah," she said in a somewhat relieved tone.

"But I've seen you eat," I said, frowning.

"It doesn't do anything. It's like eating air. And it doesn't taste good either," she said, still sounding annoyed but a bit more at ease. "The only thing that is truly satisfying is human blood. Animal blood works ... For a little bit. It's not satisfying but it will sustain you for a bit. Also tastes like shit, though." She sat back down once again, looking miserable. She locked eyes with me. "I'm sorry I got you into this mess," she said mournfully. "I ... I don't know how to fix it."

"So am I just destined to inevitability get killed by you?"

"Yes," she said, looking away, "but I don't want to. I want you to ... live your life like you did before your accident. As if all of this never happened. But it's irreversible. Either I do it or you will kill yourself. You can't just walk out of a vampire curse. Besides, humans are not supposed to know we exist. That's another guaranteed way to die. That is why Ubel put so much effort in exposing me to you."

"So I'm triple dead," I said, while looking down at my broken leg. It was silent for a while. "Well, for what it's worth, it was a wild ride," I joked, Bluebell just grinned dryly. "Does that mean that us hanging out was all just ... because of a curse?"

"At first," said Bluebell shyly. "You found me, and you wanted to be around me for that reason. I just tried to keep you safe. It was all chemical then, and I guess it still is for you, but I have really enjoyed our time together."

"Well, me too," I said.

She shook her head. "Maybe, but it's not voluntarily," she said, sounding a bit down. "I hope we can find a way to just have everything go back to how it was so you can be happy again."

I wanted to argue, to say I was feeling happy, but I was sitting in an ice-cold bunker with a broken leg, a near-death experience and a skeleton in a corner. Despite everything, I enjoyed Bluebell's company. I decided not to argue. I had no idea how everything would continue.

"How did this all start?" I asked. "Were you ... born like this?"

"No, vampires aren't birthed. They are made."

"When did you become one?"

"I, uhm, I don't think I want to talk about it," she said as she looked down at the ground. "It's a long story."

"Right ..." I said. I looked up at the latch, and then a thought popped into my head. "So ... how would one turn into a vampire?"

She looked at me with a slightly disapproving look. "Are you implying something?"

"That could be the solution, right? You wouldn't have to kill me, just ... turn me into one, however that works. Everyone wins."

She looked offended. "No one wins. Vampires aren't alive."

"Well, you ..."

She just shook her head. "Don't glorify this, please. I would have never chosen this life if I had the choice and you're not in the position to make a decision like that."

I frowned. "What you mean by that?"

"I don't mean that in a bad way," she said. "But ... a choice like that needs to be well-informed, without being influenced by a curse and despair. Besides, I don't know if I could do it."

I thought about it dreamily. It seemed like an interesting world, full of fantasy. Bluebell snapped me out of it.

"Junie, the only meat you eat is made from soy. I bet you're mad that you had to ride a flying horse here. How in the world could you think that being a bloodsucking predator is fun?"

She made a fair point.

"You should rest," she said, ending the conversation. "I asked Rosa to get you some food."

She made a hand gesture towards the bag with food that I still hadn't touched.

"That's considerate, thank you."

I couldn't help but look at the pile of bones once again.

"Oh no, I'm so sorry," she said as she followed my gaze. "I'll take them out right away. You stay here and eat something, okay? I'll bring Rosa in, she should rest too."

She made her way over to the pile of bones and lifted them up, making it look like an everyday activity such as taking the trash out.

"Don't you need to rest too?"

She stuck out her arm that had previously been full of wounds, but was now covered in what looked like scar tissue. I hadn't even noticed it.

"How?"

"We heal fast," she said, matter-of-factly. "I'll be right outside. Get some rest."

Then she jumped up, bust out the latch and disappeared, the heavy latch falling back into place.

Chapter Fourteen

Endora

It was the next day in Bluebell's bunker. After I had called my parents and told them we had taken an earlier flight and didn't have time to say goodbye (they just barely believed it, especially since all of our stuff was still packed at home), I had finally started to eat some of the food that was in the bag. I was grateful for the food, the lamp and the flashlight that Rosabella had gotten for me, but unfortunately neither she nor Bluebell seemed to have realized that the bunker was too cold for a human to be comfortable so I ended up wearing some of Bluebell's clothes over mine to try and stay warm. Rosabella had done pretty good on the food, I thought. She got cereal and soy drink, bread and some chips. She also got instant noodles and soups but unfortunately nothing to prepare it with, so eating warm food wasn't going to happen. She also got bottled water, and even some bamboo bowls, plates and cutlery that Bluebell hadn't thought of. Fortunately, Rosabella had also brought some painkillers so I wasn't in constant pain from my leg.

With not much to do, I spent the day napping, reading Bluebell's nature magazines with the flashlight and talking to Rosabella. I thought that the magazines were a tad boring, but I felt like boring was nice at this point. Napping was unpleasant on the hard floor. Talking with Rosabella was fun, but even that couldn't go on forever.

Being underground without any light from the outside, the only way of knowing what the time was, was by using my phone. The battery was lasting still since I hadn't been using it, partly because of realizing that there was no power whatsoever in Bluebell's bunker and I didn't have any means of charging it. When I looked at the time after what seemed like forever it was about nine at night. I felt relieved that the long day was coming to an end, but then I realized that it would probably mean that the chances of getting attacked were increasing, since the sun was about to set.

"Is there any way of knowing when they'll come looking for us?"

Rosabella opened her eyes, it looked like she had been napping sitting up against the wall.

"Any time after sunset. But they won't come in here, you're safe as long as you stay inside."

"I know but ... they could attack you or Bluebell when you're outside watching, right?"

I got confused by my own question for a second. Why didn't we all just stay in the bunker then?

"Bluebell wants to attack Devlin to put an end to all this," Rosabella explained, noticing my puzzled expression. "He can't come inside because it's her territory. He will smell you and come look for you. Before he can retreat, realizing it's a dead end for him, Bluebell will attack him."

"How do you know Ubel won't come with him?"

"Ubel is a coward." She chuckled. "He lets others do his dirty work for him. He wouldn't risk it."

"Wasn't this Devlin's vendetta?" I asked, confused. "Why is he meddling to begin with?"

"Because he is a prick. He tries to act like he's looking out for Devlin but really he just wants to taunt Bluebell. It's his favourite thing."

"I see ..." I said. "But ... can Bluebell win, fighting Devlin?"

"Yes," Rosabella said confidently. "Devlin is strong but inexperienced. Bluebell is strong, experienced and smart. Now she's rested and fed, when they fought before she was already at a disadvantage because they had weakened her but she still managed to get away."

The thought of it worried me. The fighting had been brutal. Plus, Rosabella had helped her get away. I had no trouble believing that Bluebell was strong, she was the one who indirectly broke my leg when she pushed me. I also had no trouble believing she was smart, seeing how well she could hide her true self, how much self-control she had and how she always thought everything through. But Devlin … He was just berserk. He was sadistic. He had no humanity, for lack of a better term.

"Is she gonna stay outside all night?"

Rosabella nodded. "Don't forget that she doesn't sleep."

"Right," I said, realizing I hadn't even considered that before.

That was why there was not a single piece of furniture here, no bed, no blankets. This bunker was a mere hiding spot and a storage unit.

"Imagine having that much time," I said, going over the idea.

"I think she'd be more than happy to switch with you."

"Willow?" an unfamiliar voice outside suddenly asked, clear enough to hear inside the bunker, though faint but sounding nervous. She must've been standing right above the bunker. "I've come to …"

Her sentence was interrupted by a loud shriek, one that reminded me of the shrieks I had heard before in the former drug lab. This shriek was a lot more agonizing, even if I didn't think that was possible.

It was as if I heard loud bangs upstairs, as if someone was loudly stomping around or throwing heavy things around. Rosabella and I were both looking up at the latch, wondering what on earth could be going on. It didn't last long enough for us to figure out. The banging stopped as quickly as it had started and it went quiet. It stayed quiet.

"I'm gonna have a look," Rosabella said.

I nodded, looking at the ground as my mind raced, and when I looked up she was already gone. I heard muffled voices from above and wondered what could be going on. Then the latch opened and I saw Rosabella's head reappear.

"You can come and get some fresh air if you want, I don't think they'll be coming back soon."

"Uhm, okay," I said, looking at her puzzled, also having no idea how to get out.

I instinctively grabbed the flashlight. Without saying a word Bluebell dropped back into the bunker, grabbed me and then jumped out again and put me down. She silently walked away from me. I tried to see where she was going but Rosabella stepped in front of me.

"I don't think you should see this. Let's go take a walk in the other direction. I'll join you."

"No," I protested. "I want to see."

"Let her," said Bluebell. Rosabella sighed and stepped aside.

I shined the flashlight and saw Bluebell sitting on the ground. She was looking at something. I started limping in her direction, my leg still hurting me, and the closer I got the more I understood why Rosabella had discouraged me. Bluebell was looking at what used to be a person.

Well, a vampire, I thought, silently admitting to myself that it all had to be real.

It was the body, and severed head, of what had been a girl who looked about the same age as me and Bluebell. She had been torn to shreds. She was bleeding the same dark substance that vampires seemed to bleed. It was too thick to form a puddle. It looked like goo. Goo mixed with chunks, the colours ranging from dark red to jet black, among shreds and shreds of torn, white flesh and broken bones. Her eyes, white and dead as all the others, were wide open and her mouth showed her fangs, her gums and her tongue that were ... a purplish grey. Her expression was that of pure fear. All of her was lying among the shreds of an olive-green outfit. Nothing was left of her. I dropped down next to Bluebell, unable to kneel. She said nothing but just stared blankly at what was left of the body.

"Who is this?"

"Endora," she said saddened.

"I heard her call your name."

"Yeah, she didn't come here to fight. I think she wanted to show me something. Or give me something."

"How come?"

"Because they tore her to shreds," she said. "She was wearing a small bag ... It was around her neck, hidden under her clothes.

They took it. She just walked up here and called for me. She knew I was here. I was hiding in a tree. Before I could react I saw Devlin and some of the others coming out of the woods. They didn't waste a second."

My eyes went over Endora's remains.

"She knew she was in danger. She looked so nervous," Bluebell continued.

Bluebell spoke of her in a very different way than she did Devlin and Ubel. She sounded nostalgic, caring, truly hurt that something had happened to this girl, even if she was another vampire.

"Who is she?"

"She is one of my oldest sisters." I remembered Bluebell despised calling Devlin and Ubel her family. It didn't seem so hard with Endora. "She stayed with Ubel and the rest when I left ... but she tried to look out for me when we lived together," she said lovingly. "She was too scared to come with me. They got inside her head. Apparently she was starting to feel a different way."

"What if it was a warning?" said Rosabella as she started to walk towards us.

Bluebell still had the same empty stare in her eyes but seemed to think she was onto something. "You may be right ..." she said. "There were four of them. They could easily take her on with just two of them or even just one of the strong ones. Maybe they were showing off."

Rosabella nodded.

"They think I'm a traitor for leaving, and liking humans ... But I try to keep to myself, for this exact reason," Bluebell explained to me. "They are relentless. Endora must have crossed Ubel in some way."

"Bluebell, they now also know that Junie is kept in your territory. They are gonna come up with a plan to lure her out."

"They are going to try to kill me," Bluebell concluded, resulting in raised eyebrows from both Rosabella and me.

"You? How come?" I asked.

"They'll kill me to get to you. You know too much, they'll do anything to get to you."

"They would kill one of their own just for that?"

Bluebell looked at me as if I was stupid once again but then she looked away and just nodded. "If they kill me you'd be forced to come out of the bunker eventually."

"And who is *they*?" I asked confused. "You said there were more who did this. Who else would do this?"

"Ubel has a big family, he has many allies. He'll send anyone he can. Besides, now that you're in on our existence, other vampires won't hesitate to come for you either."

"What about you, Rosabella? Can you help?"

"I can't kill vampires," Rosabella said, "but they can kill me. They'd be glad to as well, since I'm helping Bluebell. They hate my guts. I won't be of much help."

"Yeah," said Bluebell, "well, let's give Endora a proper ceremony. Then we can think about what to do next."

"Like a funeral?" I asked curiously.

"Kind of," Bluebell answered. "We'll burn her remains. Can't risk a human accidentally digging up a vampire one day. Besides, vampire venom is not something you want in the soil."

Rosabella started walking away.

"Are you okay?" I asked Bluebell.

"Never better," she said with a snicker. "Let's go help Rosa find some wood."

Rosabella tried to keep me from being present at the burning but Bluebell insisted I stayed so I did.

Bluebell said her words of goodbye and then started the fire.

It was not like I expected it to be. When the fire got to Endora's body, it was like the flames just ate her up. There wasn't a smell you'd expect from burning someone, there was no smoke; in fact, the smoke from the burning wood seemed to disappear right with Endora's remains, vanishing into thin air. It was like she just faded out of existence. Like she never died, or never even lived.

But at the very last moment, when Bluebell and Rosabella already had thought that the ceremony was over, there was smoke again, and something started to smell. It was a smell that made my stomach turn at instant and made me want to vomit.

"Bluebell, get inside, now!" Rosabella suddenly said, sounding panicked. Without saying a word Bluebell ran to the latch and dropped in. "It can't be …" Rosabella whispered to herself. "Quick, help me put out the fire."

Rosabella thought for a second and then ran off again, having come back with a bunch of rocks that she threw into the fire so it became smaller. I started looking around for some as well, clumsily holding the flashlight in my one hand and grabbing rocks with the other, while simultaneously trying not to put too much pressure on my leg, and threw them in. When the flames were small enough she started stomping them out. She waited until they had completely died out and there were just some embers among the rocks which she then started to remove.

Underneath the rocks, among the burned up wood was something that had been blackened by the flames but was still somewhat intact. Rosabella picked it up and just stared at it.

"Is that … a heart?" I said, nauseous beyond belief and wanting to gag at the sight of it.

She nodded. "It is a heart," she said in disbelief. She looked up at me and back to the burned organ.

"It should've vanished with the rest of the body," she said with raised eyebrows. "She … She was becoming human again."

I stared at her dumbstruck. "You can do that?"

"No," Rosabella said and chuckled. "There are many who are … enemies of vampires, for many reasons. Some of them try to make potions to try to hunt and kill them. There are also those who see it as a remedy, a potion for those who wish to become human again. But no one has been able to make such a potion yet."

"Ever?"

"As far as we know," Rosabella answered, "but it looks like we might have been wrong."

She looked back at the heart once again.

"I … need to go bury this. You go back to the bunker with Bluebell."

I nodded. She walked with me to the latch and she helped me back in, Bluebell catching me as I had to drop down. Then Rosabella went off into the woods with the heart in her hands.

Bluebell helped me to sit and then she sat down against the wall herself, looking at me with curiosity.

"Rosabella said she was becoming human again, that she took some type of potion."

"Do you know how long I've been looking for a potion like that?" she asked, fascinated.

I shook my head.

"Well … You wouldn't believe me if I told you anyway," she said as she looked away, "but it's been long." I realized that I hadn't given thought to that either. Who knows how long she might have been twenty three, like she told me.

"Maybe she came to tell you," I suggested.

"Maybe," she agreed.

"She could've been carrying some more of it with her before they stole it."

"Could be … it's just a little weird."

"Why?"

"Endora was a good person, she deserved a better family than Ubel and his kin, but she loved being a vampire."

"Oh," was all I said. I didn't know that was an option, I realized. Bluebell loathed being a vampire and seemed to have a heart of gold. I assumed Devlin and Ubel loved being vampires, and they were horrific.

"She loved how strong she was, the security of immortality, not having to sleep, all that. She enjoyed it."

Then Bluebell frowned. "So, I don't understand why she would use such a potion."

I looked around the bunker, thinking. "What if … she knew Devlin would be coming after her to steal it, or whatever she was carrying, and she needed to be sure she could show you that it existed?"

"Yeah, but why? She could have just come talk to me without any of it with her. I could get some of it myself."

I hummed in response, she made a good point.

"Either way ... we don't have that much time to ruminate. When Rosa is back I'm going to go and find some allies."

"Allies?"

"Devlin will not come alone. I need help."

"So you're really going to fight them again?"

"You think I'm just going to deliver you to them?"

"No, but ... You also said it was inevitable that I would have to die."

She stared at me dumbstruck for a second.

"You almost sound like you *want* to die."

"Of course not! I just ... I don't know. Sometimes it feels like I should've just died at the accident."

"Don't say that!"

"But it's true." I continued, "Then there would be no curse at all. None of this would have happened. Apparently I have to die anyway."

"I won't just let you die, Junie, there has to be a way. Besides," she said, realizing, "if I can get that potion then I can become human again and then the curse will be lifted. We could just live normally."

"Oh yeah," I said and smiled at last. "I guess you're right."

"I could even get a house," she mused.

"But if you become human ... that means you're going to die as well, doesn't it?"

"Of course. But that is part of life," she said and smiled at me. "I'd rather live out my life as a human and then die like it's supposed to be. Death doesn't scare me."

I nodded in understanding, although, thinking about Bluebell giving up her immortality and eventually dying did make me feel a bit sad.

What did make me happy, however, was the thought that Bluebell now had a reason to fight, beyond wanting to keep me alive. She wanted to fight for her life as a human, to live life the way *she* wanted. That thought comforted me.

Chapter Fifteen

Peripeteia

It was the second morning of waking up in Bluebell's bunker, leaving my back and neck sore. I felt stiff, I was still cold, and I was getting a bit antsy from the discomfort.

Bluebell had been on the phone since before I woke up, luckily having the decency to do it outside the bunker.

In between phone calls, she had explained to me that she thought there were only two types of vampires in the world. There were those who were a part of a family and those who lived more solitary lifestyles. She also explained to me that there really weren't that many of them in the world.

She estimated a population of approximately ten thousand. Compared to humanity, of course, that was nothing, but I couldn't shrug off the ominous feeling I got when I thought about there being that many vampires in the world. It was still ten thousand; ten thousand bloodthirsty beings who would kill me without a second thought.

Bluebell had been stressed the whole night as she was hoping to have some allies gathered by sunset but it hadn't been going well at all. It was now morning and she hadn't had any success.

Bluebell had a seemed to have a very different way of thinking compared to other vampires. I overheard the word 'suicide' from the other side of the line during one particular call she was making.

I wasn't sure if it was because they had considered fighting Devlin and other members of that family in a suicide mission or if they called it that because Bluebell had mentioned the potion that could turn vampires back into humans. Either way, Bluebell's mission didn't seem to spark much interest with other vampires. She mentioned that hers – or Devlin and Ubel's – family was one of the biggest in the worldwide vampire population. For that reason, a huge number of potential allies were out of the question from the start.

"But Onyx, you *loathe* Ubel!" Bluebell said as she was pacing around the bunker during a call. "This is your chance!"

Then she let out a soft sigh and looked at the ground. "Okay, call me if you change your mind. Bye."

"Even Onyx?" Rosabella asked after Bluebell had hung up.

"Even Onyx," Bluebell said and let out another sigh. I decided to keep my curiosity to myself.

Then Bluebell picked up her phone again to answer a call. "Hello? Yes, that's right, who is this? Oh, really?" she looked at us, smiling. "May I ask why? Hm-hm. I see."

I saw her smile fade and the same defeated look she had when she was looking at Endora's remains returned. She looked away.

"I am so sorry to hear that. Where are you from? All right. When can you be here? Saecula Forest. Great. Meet me at the Eastern edge. Take care and try not to draw any attention. Bye."

She hung up and exhaled deeply, then looked up at us.

"We have someone. I'm gonna go and pick her up. You stay put."

And within seconds she was up, but before the latch fell shut behind her I heard her curse.

"Shit! What ..." the rest became muffled as the latch shut.

Rosabella and I listened attentively. There was a lot of going back and forth with some raising of voices before it went silent again. The latch opened and I saw Bluebell looking in.

"Ellison and Etana are here," she said to Rosabella. She nodded in understanding. "They're staying on watch. Don't let Junie out until I'm back."

Then the latch fell shut again and she was gone.

What seemed to be a day of doom turned out to be the opposite. As evening started to fall Bluebell had been able to gather quite a following.

Bluebell filled me in on the details. Ellison and Etana were Endora's siblings; biological siblings, who had once been a human family. They all had the same blond hair, and their facial structure was clearly similar as well. They came to unite with Bluebell after finding out that Ubel had ordered their sister to be murdered. The person Bluebell met at the edge of the forest was someone named Ignacia.

She had only recently become a vampire, thanks to Ubel. Bluebell couldn't bear to say why she showed up but it had something to do with Ignacia's family. Then there were a few who came over from Invicta – Bluebell had recently visited them on her vacation there. They had a similar mind-set to Bluebell; they also wished they had a choice when they were bitten (although they didn't seem to suffer from self-loathing); and they were working on a potion as well. The majority who had showed up were from rival families who had long standing feuds with the family Bluebell came from. A few of the more solitary living vampires had shown up as well.

The very last person who showed up was someone from Ubel's family, a woman named Fallax, who somehow looked nothing short of a warrior even if she had big doe eyes. She told Bluebell that she had recently been bitten, against her will, and wanted to get back at him.

At the end of the day, I was surrounded by a total of twenty-six vampires and a shapeshifter sitting in the dark, cold bunker with only Bluebell, afraid of what was to come. The powerlessness was eating away at me.

Bluebell was sitting across from me, watching me eat corn-flakes in the dim light.

"Quite a turnout," I commented between bites.

She nodded. "I'm glad. Many of them I don't even know, they're just happy to fight Ubel and his minions."

"Maybe they just needed the push."

"Maybe. Well, it worked. They're ready to go." I smiled faintly.

"You have no idea how restless everyone is just because of your presence down here," she said and grinned. "If only you knew."

"What's it like?"

She widened her eyes. "I wouldn't know how to explain. It's irresistible when it's in front of you. Kind of like an addiction, I guess."

I frowned. "That sounds hard. You seem to be doing pretty well, though."

"Yeah," she chuckled.

"Blue ... I hope you're gonna be okay after all this. And I'm sorry about your sister. She sounded really great."

"She had a good heart," she said, then she laughed. "That sounded more inappropriate than I intended."

I laughed awkwardly with her, the image still clear as day in my mind.

"She did. Good fashion sense too."

"I guess," she chuckled.

"That outfit was gorgeous," I continued, thinking about the shreds that had surrounded her, "from what I could see from what was left ... that olive green ..."

Suddenly Bluebell lifted her eyes and stared me dead in the eye as if I just confessed something horrible.

"What?" I asked while holding a spoonful of cornflakes above my bowl.

She just kept staring for a while longer and then she dropped her gaze and stared at the ground, wide-eyed.

"Are you okay?"

She didn't respond. I put my bowl down, got up and dropped down next to her. I put my hand on her shoulder, which felt cold and hard.

"Blue?"

"Yes," she said, her mind clearly somewhere else. "I'm fine, it's just ... what you said."

She slid my hand off her shoulder.

"What are you talking about?"

"Olive," she mumbled, then she started getting up. "I have to talk to Ellison en Etana. I'll send Rosa." She went outside.

A few moments later Rosabella joined me in the bunker, flying in as a little bird and then changing into a full-grown human woman right in front of me.

"Is she okay?" I asked with a worried look on my face.

"Has Bluebell ever told you anything about her family?" she asked as she sat down close to me.

"Well, I know that Ubel is supposed to be her father and …" I stopped talking because she shook her head impatiently.

"Her biological family."

"Huh?" I realized at that moment that she had never mentioned anything about them at all.

"I don't know much either, she doesn't talk about them a lot," she responded, "but she told me once that she lived with her parents and her little brother until she was bitten. She loved her family. Especially her brother. But logically, she couldn't exactly stay in touch afterwards. That was a long time ago."

I nodded, although not sure I saw the connection.

"Her brother was called Oliver."

"*Oh*, the olive clothes," I thought aloud. "Endora. Does she think it has anything to do with her brother?" Rosabella nodded. "Isn't that a bit far − fetched?"

"She would have to be subtle if she wanted to get her message across without Ubel finding out."

"I guess that is true … When was she … bitten?"

"I can't tell you exactly, but Oliver should be long dead by now. It's impossible he survived this long."

"Unless he was bitten as well," I concluded.

"Right. That could explain why Endora took that potion. She knew that she would be killed. She had probably found something out that she shouldn't have. Whatever she was carrying with her must have been important and she wanted to ensure that even if it got stolen, and if she died, Bluebell would still be able to figure out what she came here for."

Chapter Sixteen

Carnage

Bluebell came back into the bunker one more time before night truly fell, to make sure I was okay and to tell me what was going to happen. Rosabella would stay down with me in the bunker; she said that I needed a distraction and someone to comfort me. I was anxious about what was about to come but she ensured me that I was safe inside the bunker, since it was an ancient vampire rule that trespassing was out of the question.

"Will you be okay out there?" I asked Bluebell.

She was more restless than I had ever seen her and was anxiously pacing around. "I don't know," she admitted, "but I have to be."

"Rosabella told me about your brother."

"Yeah. I'm not holding back."

"Do you really think he could be alive?" I asked.

"I- Well, he shouldn't be. But Endora was sending a message. She knew something. It has to be about him."

"Can I ask how along ago you …"

"Turned?"

"Yeah."

"Do you really want to know?" she asked cautiously.

"I do."

She grinned. "Well, I was born in sixteen hundred and one. Bitten in sixteen hundred and twenty-four."

I stared at her dumbfounded for a solid ten seconds.

"You asked," she said and laughed.

I did. But I couldn't believe it. For now, I was just trying to make it through this situation, I figured, and I'd worry about the insanity of it all later.

"What was it like then?"

"Tons of castles, people dressed in fancy clothes, obsessions with royals, cruelty; a lot of cruelty. People weren't as civilized then," she said as she stared into the distance and chuckled, "and not so sanitary either. Disease was everywhere. It was all very different. You wouldn't recognize Cunabula if you saw what it looked like back then."

"Do you ever miss it?"

Suddenly, she seemed very interested in the muffled voices outside and not in my question. "I should probably go out there. It's almost midnight," she said as she got up.

I looked at her and I couldn't help but feel afraid. *What if she didn't come back?*

"Promise me that you won't try to get out. I will come to you once it's safe. Don't go outside," she said.

I nodded. We looked each other in the eye for a moment.

"Oh, I should probably take these out," she said as she turned away. She then started looking for a container and swiftly took out her contacts and put them inside the container with some contact fluid.

"Sorry," she apologized shyly. "They are restricting."

"Be careful," I told her.

She nodded. She looked at me one last time, smiled and made her way outside. I felt my heart drop the moment she left.

A few moments later, Rosabella came back to sit with me. She said nothing, but she also looked afraid and a little tense. We chatted awkwardly for a bit, rather than just sitting in silence, but we soon heard signs of a fight starting, and we both looked up startled. There were no voices; only muffled sounds of what sounded like screaming. Once again, the same eerie screeches I had heard before. There was also stomping. There were thuds that sounded like people being thrown. I was happy that most of the sounds were faint, but even so, they were extremely unsettling and anxiety inducing.

"Right, I'm going to try to keep you distracted, Junie, talk to me."

"Uhm, okay, I, uhm ..." I was interrupted by a loud sound right above us, it sounded as if someone fell right on top of the hatch.

Rosabella moved over to sit right across from me, as close as she could, so I was facing her.

"Why don't we take this time to talk about all the new information you got these past days? I'm sure you have lots of questions."

I simply nodded.

"Were you a believer in mythical creatures and such before all this happened?"

Another bang in the background, further away this time. I shook my head.

"I found it fascinating to read about and stuff ... but I never believed they were real. It still feels surreal now."

"I imagine it must be odd."

"Were you ... born like this?"

Rosabella nodded. "Shapeshifters are very different from vampires. We are born like this and can't turn people like vampires do."

Another loud thud, followed by a scream.

"So ... does that mean you're mortal?" I asked; doing my best to ignore everything outside.

"Yes, we live longer than humans do but we do die. The oldest among us would be about three hundred years old now, but she doesn't have much time left."

"How old are you?"

"One hundred and eighty-seven."

"Wow," I said, taking Bluebell's earlier revelation of her being more than four hundred years old into account. "You guys must have really seen some stuff."

The sounds outside started to become louder, as if the fight were intensifying. I felt grateful that the bunker muted the outside noises so much.

"Do you think they are okay out there?" I asked, not able to ignore it any longer when a loud scream emerged from right on top of the bunker.

"I hope so ... They are outnumbered."

"They are? By how many?"

119

"I– I don't know, I saw every single one of Ubel's children out there that I know of … and even some I've never seen before. It seems like they are all here except Ubel."

"He sent everyone?! How many of them are there?"

"I don't know but it's quite a lot," she admitted. "I have no idea how they're going to win this."

We both fell silent for a moment; the battle sounds outside seeming more frightening than before now that even Rosabella had admitted her worries. It also sounded like the fight was becoming more intense by the minute. Having admitted her own fears, it seemed like Rosabella's attempt to distract me was over. She looked like she was on the verge of tears but was trying not to show it.

Eventually, after what seemed like an eternity, the bangs and screams outside became fainter and fainter and the fight seemed to die out. At last, when it seemed completely silent, Rosabella cleared her throat.

"I, uhm, I'm going to go and have a look," she said awkwardly. She disappeared into a small, black dot once again and then seemed to just disappear completely. I stared at the latch in confusion for a moment until I heard footsteps above me and I figured she had to have turned into something minuscule to get out of the bunker.

A while later, I woke up from the slumber I had fallen into when Rosabella had left.

"She's okay," she said and smiled, suddenly back to sitting with me. I couldn't help but smile too.

I honestly wasn't expecting any good news. We sat in silence while she took the time to process what had happened up there and that the person she was guarding was fine. She also seemed to be puzzled about something, but she didn't speak.

I found out what it was later that night, or morning, as I was woken up again by the light of sunrise beaming in once Bluebell opened the latch to return to the bunker. She looked worse than I'd ever seen her, even worse than when Ubel and Devlin had kidnapped her. Her clothes were shredded, tons of what looked like old, oxidized blood was all over her and trails and smudges of dried but fresh blood were around her mouth and on her chin and throat. Somehow, she looked beaten and yet simultaneously satisfied. I could see new scar tissue all over her but whatever wounds had been inflicted on her must have closed already. Her eyes were still white, hands still un-gloved, and her teeth were larger than I'd seen them yet – it must've been past the time slot of when she'd usually file them. She looked like what clearly was her natural self – her natural self who had just come back from hunting. She rushed to one of the corners of the bunker, grabbed some stuff out of a bag and started cleaning herself. When she turned back around, her face and body were cleared of blood, and she went to change into clothing that looked presentable and not dark red. At last, she put her signature blue contacts back in and started brushing her hair. If it weren't for her fangs, dirty nails and the paleness that was just a tad too pale to be a simple lack of pigment, she almost looked like a normal woman in her twenties. I only then noticed that her nose wasn't crooked anymore.

She flicked a piece of chewing gum into her mouth and started cleaning her nails, paying no attention to the excessive scar tissue all over her body. It was like she didn't feel any of it.

She cast a look at some tool that was lying on the ground but decided that now was not the time. She walked over to Rosabella and me, who had been looking at her the entire time, to finally talk to us.

"You're okay!" It came out of my mouth before I knew it.

"Yeah, I guess I am," she said, sounding confused.

I raised an eyebrow. "Huh?"

"They … they started fighting each other. It didn't make sense … But it helped, most of us got off pretty well."

"Most? Who didn't?" I asked.

"Ignacia and Fallax," she said, as she looked down in remorse. "They were just too young."

I was confused for a moment, thinking that Ignacia was obviously older than Bluebell was and Fallax couldn't be *that* much younger than her either. Then I realized that she must've meant the period they had spent as a vampire since both had only recently been bitten.

"I shouldn't have let them fight," she said mournfully.

"Nonsense, Bluebell, they made their choice," Rosabella said.

"*Did* they?" she suddenly snapped. "Fallax wanted justice and Ignacia ..." She couldn't bear to look at us for some reason. "She had her reasons. It wasn't much of a choice either," she said as she glared at Rosabella. Rosabella seemed to have decided that it was best not to respond.

"So, what about ... your, well, Ubel's family? What happened to them?"

Bluebell's expression changed for the better. "Well, like I said they suddenly started to attack each other ... It was the weirdest thing. Eventually we didn't even have to fight them anymore, they were just taking themselves out."

"Why would they do that?"

"They had taken the potion," she said as she frowned in confusion. "All of them. Their hearts were beating blood again. So, they started to attack each other because they couldn't control themselves."

The three of us all had a confused expression on our faces. Why on earth would all of them have taken the potion that was practically an anti-vampire antidote? It would send them straight to their grave, smelling like blood among a group of raging vampires while being mortal.

"Devlin got away," Bluebell said bitterly. "When the smell started to permeate the air he was already gone. He fled right away."

"So, he was the only one who hadn't taken it?" asked Rosabella.

"No ... I could smell the trail he left. He also took it. I think that's why he ran; he knew he didn't stand a chance. He'd be smelling of blood and be outnumbered."

"Why didn't you follow him?" I asked, almost offended. Devlin was the entire reason this had happened, or at least half the reason. He shouldn't be able to just get away.

"Because it was a trap," concluded Rosabella.

Bluebell nodded. I didn't understand what that meant at all.

"Ubel wanted them dead," she started. "He must've had them ingest the potion somehow without them knowing. I think he wanted to make sure that there wasn't another traitor and to just exterminate them all. He sent them on a suicide mission."

I felt my stomach turn. Killing all your children, as he called them … because of a precaution?

He was even crueller than I thought.

"Even Devlin?" I asked in disbelief.

"He doesn't care about Devlin, Devlin cares about him. He'd do anything for him, that's the only reason Ubel favours him. He once favoured me too." She chuckled, "it's out of convenience."

"But why was it a trap? He wanted them dead, and they died, except for Devlin. Weren't they the ones who were lured into a trap?"

"That's part of it. He wants to show off his powers. He won't rest until you're dead," Bluebell said as she looked back at me. "It's not over."

"But what now?" asked Rosabella. "How do we proceed?"

"We have a proper ceremony and bury the hearts. Then I'll hunt some more and then maybe you can go and get something to charge Junie's phone with, so her parents don't lose their shit; and get something proper for her to eat. After that I have to go and look for Ubel and Devlin." Bluebell saw the concerned look on my face. "I have no choice, Junie," she said. "I have to look for him."

Rosabella and I both knew she was talking about Oliver. I couldn't bear to say that I still thought it was a bit far-fetched.

"And I have to get my hands on that potion," she said as she was eyeing me.

"But she would still know too much," said Rosabella with concern, "giving her that potion would only get rid of one problem."

"I know," said Bluebell as she frowned, "I haven't figured that part out yet."

If anyone could figure it out, it would be Bluebell, but there wasn't a solution. I felt like I had no choice but to go along with

Bluebell's decisions. If I went outside, I would be killed for sure. The only chance I had of survival was with her, staying in her bunker. I could only hope it all worked out for the best and that she would stick to her guns.

Chapter Seventeen

Trespassing

A little later that morning we went outside to have the ceremony, as Bluebell called it. She and Rosabella performed it while I sat near the fire, observing. The ceremony consisted of burning over a hundred vampire bodies and having them fade into thin air, except for their hearts, that unlike the rest of their bodies, were strangely human. Bluebell didn't run away this time, being aware of what had happened to the others wasn't meant to be some secret weapon from Devlin and Ubel sent to kill her. It was at a time like this that it was very convenient to be around someone who had the ability to transform into any living creature so she could dig a hole that was deep enough to bury many hearts in without it being noticeable.

It was a completely desolate area, though, so neither Bluebell nor Rosabella were worried about us or the bodies being seen, but of course they couldn't take the risk and just leave them lying around.

Ignacia and Fallax's bodies were burnt last; fading into the morning sunlight as if they never existed, including their hearts. Rosabella was taking care of the turned-human hearts in the meantime.

While their bodies turned to air, not even dust, Bluebell closed her eyes and hummed a melody that was unfamiliar to me, but I thought sounded hauntingly beautiful.

"Oliver used to sing to me when we were young," she said as she opened her eyes at last, now looking at just a fire burning with no trace of any person left.

"It sounded beautiful," I said as I gave her an assuring smile. "You never told me how it happened."

"What?"

125

"How you were … bitten. Anything from your past, really."

"I told you when I was born." She chuckled, "and how it was."

"You talked about castles and hygiene for five seconds! That is not talking!"

"Fine," she said and rolled her eyes. "I'll give you three questions."

I pursed my lips and thought hard. "Well … how were you bitten? And don't say with teeth." Bluebell snorted. "I mean, sketch me an image. What was the situation?"

She let out a soft sigh before she started, clearly not looking forward to talking about this. She stared into the dying fire.

"I was standing in the garden, alone. My family was inside. Suddenly…" she frowned slightly. "Someone else came into the garden. I had no idea where he came from. It was Ubel."

"Did he … look like he does now?"

"Yeah, nothing's changed. He just showed up out of nowhere and didn't even try to cover up what he looked like. I thought he was some sicko that was coming to kill me. He just smiled with his giant teeth exposed." She spoke with a tone of disgust to her voice, "and the next thing I knew I was on the ground, paralysed. It hurt so much. I wanted to scream but I just … couldn't. I just lay there, whimpering. Everything was blurry and I thought I was going to pass out but I didn't. I wished I could. He was just standing there, still smiling and I saw that his lips and teeth were red and there was blood dripping from them. I could comprehend that he had bitten me, but of course I didn't know what on earth he would do that for and why it hurt so bad. This was before everyone started accusing everyone and their mother of vampirism, so I didn't really understand."

She went silent for a bit. I had been wondering what it would feel like, and what exactly made it hurt so much, but I was also imagining Bluebell, at the same age as she was now, with the exact same look, except that she would look *alive*, in excruciating pain on the ground.

"After what felt like forever, my parents found me and took me to the hospital. Mind you, hospitals then weren't that … advanced.

Of course, they couldn't figure out what was wrong with me. By the time I got to the hospital they couldn't find anything on me. I guess the bite mark had already gone. My eyes turned white. My skin got pale. Unhealthy pale. Eventually my heart stopped beating and I stopped breathing but I wasn't dead. The doctors were mortified. They didn't know what to do and they were scared it was contagious, so they put me in isolation. After a while, I started feeling great, weird as that may sound. I felt so energized but so restless. I was hungry. By the time I got out I looked even worse." She pulled a faint grin, as if to laugh at her own misery. "My teeth had grown at least an inch. The damage was done."

I took it all in while once again staring at the fire that was now just ashes and burned wood.

"That must have been terrifying," I concluded softly.

"Yeah," she said, as if she had already said way too much. "It was."

I looked at her, at her pasty skin, the deep scars that were open wounds not so long before, her bright blue eyes that got their colour from contact lenses and I grieved for a moment for the girl that was once flesh and blood and was now stuck in a life she didn't choose.

"I don't want this for you," she said and met my gaze with sorrow.

I just nodded and pushed myself up with great effort. I went in for a hug. As usual, it wasn't a warm, comforting hug. It wouldn't be if she tried. Even if she was shaped like a human, it felt as if I was embracing a statue. She inhaled deeply and let go. She gazed into the cloudy sky.

"I, uhm, I have to go and hunt. After I'm back Rosa will get you your stuff."

I looked over and saw that Rosabella had finished burying the hearts and was once again looking like a middle aged, brunette woman, albeit with mud all over her.

She and Bluebell helped me back inside the bunker and Rosabella and I sat down as Bluebell set off deep into the woods. Rosabella started wiping the mud off herself and sighed in exhaustion.

"So, what do you want me to get for you?" she asked as she pulled out a cleansing wipe out of a package that was lying around.

"Anything that has fruits and veggies, please," I answered.

She nodded. "You and Bluebell are very similar," she said with a grin, sounding a bit surprised. "I'll find you something nutritious."

"Thank you. And maybe some sanitary stuff or something that smells good," I added. "I have never wanted to shower this much."

Of course, there was no shower in the bunker, and it didn't make me feel good. As I started thinking about all the lovely smelling soaps I had waiting for me at home, I started noticing a subtle, sweet but slightly chemical smell in the bunker that was unfamiliar to me.

I looked over at Rosabella and saw she was using some cream on her skin.

"What is in there?" I asked curiously.

"Some kind of flower," she answered as she looked at the packaging with curiosity.

"Can I have some too?"

"Sure," she said and she smiled at me faintly.

She walked over to me and reached her hand out with the small container in it. I reached out and took it.

I woke up with a severe headache and found myself spread out on the floor of the bunker. I lifted my head with difficulty and looked around. Rosabella was lying on the floor as well, the container she had been holding also on the floor, the glass now cracked. The smell was still present, but it wasn't as strong. It seemed to be fading away.

"Rosa?" I asked, barely producing any sound. She didn't respond.

I sat up with difficulty and as I did, I noticed a sharp pain in my left arm. Frowning and squinting, from now having two painful limbs, I stretched out my arm and looked at it. I instantly gasped. On my arm were bite marks. Deep, bleeding bite marks. Looking at it I felt myself getting dizzy, sweaty and anxious. Thinking about it I realized that I was feeling dizzy and hot to begin with. I put my right hand to my head and noticed that I was burning up.

"Rosa?" I asked again, and this time Rosabella responded. She blinked a few times and looked dazed.

"Huh? What happened?" she asked.

With great difficulty I stretched out my arm to let her see. She also gasped. Just as she moved forward to get closer to me the latch flew open like it hadn't before and Bluebell jumped in, looking frantic. She walked over to me, grabbed my arm and started analysing it. Then she also put her hand up to my forehead and drew the same conclusion that I had.

"Shit … You're burning up …" she turned to Rosabella. "What happened? How did they do this?"

"I don't know … I blacked out. I just woke up."

I nodded as the same had happened to me. Bluebell looked both angry and defeated at the same time. She just let herself fall into a sitting position and stared at the tooth-shaped wounds on my arm.

"Are these vampire bites?" I whimpered.

She shook her head. "No, they stick to the rules." She stopped and hesitated for a moment. She then continued, "These are wolf bites. Werewolf bites."

"Werewolf bites?!" I said in a panic. I attempted to sit up straighter, but I fell back and flinched from the pain.

"Yes," said Bluebell mournfully.

"There are werewolves too?!" I said in an almost whiny voice.

"Yes," answered Bluebell softly. "They must have had somebody watching to see when I would be gone. It smells like chloroform in here. They must have had it spread into the bunker somehow."

"I feel sick," I said, sweating and feeling uncomfortable.

"That means it's working," she said. "Let's go get you some fresh air."

Bluebell took me outside through the latch and sat me down on the grass.

"What do you mean it's working?" I whimpered, squinting at the sunlight.

"Being bitten by a werewolf … It's a little bit like being bitten by a vampire. I mean, it works differently but it makes you one of them," she said, and looked me in the eyes as if looking for confirmation that I understood what she was trying to say.

"What's going to happen to me?"

"It was full moon last night … It'll be about a month before you … transform. But for now, you will just be sick for a few days."

"Should we clean the wound?"

"We should keep it clean and covered so nothing nasty gets in there. But lycanthropy … that's what being a werewolf is called, basically, it's already started, we can't reverse that."

Rosabella appeared near the latch, she looked ready to go.

"I'm going to get you some stuff for your arm. And some food and power … whatever it's called, to charge your phone with," she said with a hand gesture.

Bluebell and I both nodded at her, and she walked off.

"I just don't understand. Who would do this?" Bluebell said as her eerie thumb was sliding over my arm, observing the bites.

I remained silent, still in pain. I shivered when her thumb got too close to one of the bites. She looked up, noticed and went to fetch some painkillers. I took them gratefully. Afterwards she took us to sit under a big tree, out of the sun. Bluebell sat down next to me with a look of relief on her face.

"I've been wondering what the deal is with sunlight."

She smiled and looked down. "It's unpleasant. Well, painful. I don't really know how to describe it."

"Is it like being sunburned?"

She shook her head. "Have you ever burned your hand on a hot pan or something? It's like that, I suppose … but continuously, all over. It's not great."

I took a sip from the water bottle she had brought me to take the painkillers with.

"I'm sorry, Junie," said Bluebell softly. "I can't believe you've been bitten."

I just laughed. At this point I didn't even know what on earth was happening anymore.

"I don't think you realize what this means," she said. And indeed I did not. "You're never going to be the same again. You will be sick every month. You'll lose your sense of self every month and lose control for who knows how long."

"Please stop," I pleaded softly.

She looked me in the eye. I just didn't have it in me at that moment to deal with the reality of it all; that I was in grave danger, still; that I had been bitten by a creature that wasn't supposed to exist, while I was intentionally knocked out by someone; that I was hiding from a murder town, *with* a murderer, who was somehow still my friend. None of it made sense. None of it seemed real. I started to realize how hard I had been working to just keep it all together, but I forced it all back into the depths of my mind again as I took a deep breath.

"There's also a good side to this, though," said Bluebell.

"Hm?"

"Well … You're no longer human. You're free from my curse. Vampires won't want to eat you anymore and you're supposed to know about vampires. There's no reason for any of them to try to kill you now. You're free."

"I am?"

She nodded. "You can go home. You've just got to make sure that when the full moon comes, you're in the right place."

I just stared into the distance, dumbfounded for a second. "Did somebody free me on purpose?"

"It seems like it," said Bluebell. "I don't get it either. It's not the outcome I had planned but … it saves both you and me from being in danger. It's actually kind of good."

Chapter Eighteen

Rosabella had returned with a powerbank and an unnecessary charger, some alcohol wipes, bandages, some sort of wound disinfectant, more painkillers, some big, fresh smoothies, salads, nuts, fresh fruit, ready to eat sandwiches, smoothie bowls and more bottles of water. It seemed like a bit of overkill, but I wasn't going to complain. Finally, she pulled out a big, scarlet book called *Hunters of Midnight*.

"What is that?" I asked while I started to clean my wounds which stung like a thousand bees.

We were still sitting in the shade and Rosabella had joined us.

"This book contains information and history on nocturnal predators like werewolves and vampires," she answered. "Creatures that humans consider mythical, it's probably not all accurate but it might give you some insight."

"Oh, thank you!"

Rosabella gave me a warm smile. Bluebell pulled a face.

"So, what happens now? Are you going to go home?" Rosabella asked.

"I guess I should … After I feel better," I said as I still felt my head pounding through the painkillers.

"You would rather sit it out in a filthy underground bunker than in a comfortable bed with your parents around?" asked Bluebell with a raised eyebrow.

"I don't want to come back sick too, on top of breaking my leg," I answered. "Besides, it's kinda fun here."

"Weirdo," said Bluebell.

"When are you going to go after them?" I asked, my mind wandering back to the fight of the previous night.

"Tonight," she answered quickly. "I have no time to waste. Rosa will take care of you."

"Why don't I come with you?"

"Well, for one, you're sick. Two, you can't walk. Three, you're not suddenly immortal now that you got bitten. It's still dangerous."

"They won't attack me for my blood now, right? So they won't want to kill me?"

"Not for that reason, no. But still, I don't know what's going to happen there. They have my brother and for some reason they never told me. It's sick."

"Ubel and Devlin know of the bunker now," said Rosabella. "Maybe she's safer if she's with you. What if they come back and try to get her out? Besides, if she goes then I can come too. We can both protect her, and I can keep an eye on you."

"Someone chose to protect her. I don't see why they would come back now. She's no longer prey, and she's allowed to know about us."

"Do you think he'll just stop now that she's no longer human?"

Bluebell stopped to think for a moment. "Well, maybe you're right. I wouldn't put it beneath him to still try and kill her just out of spite … Do you really want to come with us, Junie?"

I nodded.

"Then we set out at midnight," she said, slightly defeated, "but we can't take risks."

We spent most of the day sitting under that same tree, enjoying the momentary peace and rest. Even though I wasn't feeling well, I ate a lot of the food Rosabella had brought back for me and shared it with her. I also managed to sleep for a few hours, enjoying the fresh, open air. Later, I eventually opened *Hunters of Midnight* and started reading the chapter on werewolves.

In folklore the werewolf, wolf walker or lycanthrope is a person with the ability to transform into a wolf, after being placed under a curse or affliction with transformations occurring on the night of the full moon.

I noticed Bluebell was reading with me over my shoulder.

"Ninety percent of this is bullshit, though," she said while scanning the pages.

"It is? Like what exactly?"

Bluebell's pasty white finger pointed to another paragraph.

There have been many different possible scenarios on how humans can transform into werewolves. By far the most common is by the bite of another werewolf. Others include drinking water from the footprint of a lycanthrope, being placed under a curse of dark magic and being born to werewolf parents.

"You can't become a werewolf by drinking from a footprint or by magic ... It's only by bites and genetics."

"So, werewolves can have werewolf babies?"

"Yes, once it's in your blood you'll pass it on if you have a child."

"Huh," I said, fascinated. "Can vampires have children too then?"

Bluebell chuckled. "No, vampire bodies are not exactly fertile. We don't even have a heartbeat."

"I'm sorry, what?"

"Yes," answered Bluebell surprised. "We do not breathe either."

I stared at her thunderstruck for a moment.

"We're called the undead for a reason."

"Hm," I remarked, fascinated. "The more you know ..."

I continued reading.

There are various remedies for lycanthropy. Exhaustion and wolfs bane have been methods used over time. Surgery, striking its forehead or scalp with a knife or piercing the hand with nails have also been used.

"Oh, I remember those times," said Bluebell with a spiteful look on her face. "So many people would be persecuted but barely any of them were actual werewolves. People would accuse anyone and anything."

"Have you met any actual werewolves then?" I asked curiously.

"Yes," answered Bluebell and Rosabella in unison. They chuckled at each other.

"They don't really live around here but there are several packs living in the Noctiluca woods."

The Noctiluca woods were located more to the North of Aspera. I had visited the place a few times for hikes and it was beautiful. But never would I have considered that something like werewolves were living in there. And in *packs*?

"They gather there at full moon. At any other time of the month they look like humans and live like humans. They do start to fall ill around the full moon and have to recover for a while after that."

"Yes, you mentioned that … Will I really be sick every month?"

"A few days before the full moon you will be sick, kind of like you are now. It'll be like a fever. Then once the full moon rises, you'll change form," Bluebell explained, "and when the sun rises again you'll change back. You will be so worn out you'll have to recover for a few days."

"What does it feel like?"

"I can't really tell you."

"Have you seen it happen?"

She nodded silently. We made eye contact and she continued hesitantly. "It seems very painful … but it happens quickly."

"What about the night itself?"

Bluebell frowned as if she wasn't sure how to answer this question. "I think it would be good for you to meet an actual werewolf so you can talk to them about all this," she said. "They can help you more than we can. Besides, it would be good for you to have a pack."

I looked at her puzzled for a second; was she telling me I should move?

"Only for the full moon nights, Junie. The rest of the time, you'll live the same life as you do now."

Chapter Nineteen

At the end of the day, I was still feeling sick, although the bites on my arm were feeling a bit better after they had been cleaned. Eating some healthy food also definitely had made me feel a bit better. Flipping once more through *Hunters of Midnight* while sitting in the bunker, reading with a flashlight, I was waiting until the sun set so I could finally go somewhere other than this one part of the forest. It now had a strange sense of comfort, though, the bunker, and the depth of the woods, but I was enthusiastic to change sceneries.

On the nights where the moon is full, lycanthropes' previously fine souls soar aimlessly through the night sky as their beast-like bodies are now to be possessed by a lust the likes of which no man will ever experience: the lust for human flesh.

It is in these nights that the beast turns against all they are on every other night of the month, where they are as you and I.

"How are you feeling?" said Rosabella, as she knelt down next to me and put the back of her hand on my forehead.

"Still a bit weak … The headache is gone, though."

"Do you need anything before we leave tonight? It won't be long."

I shook my head, which didn't hurt anymore, but it made me feel once more how sore my muscles were.

Bluebell threw some sort of bar at me from across the room and I barely managed to catch it.

"Eat this."

I unwrapped what appeared to be some sort of protein bar and started eating it.

"Thank you," I mumbled with my mouth full.

Approximately half an hour later we were all climbing out of the latch to head towards where Bluebell thought Devlin, and Ubel might be. For some reason I was handed the backpack that carried the stuff we were taking with us – which wasn't all that much.

"First, we're going to their house. I don't know if they'll be there – unless they either set a trap or want to be caught – but it's the best chance of meeting them or finding a clue."

"How far is it?" I asked, still not feeling my best and worrying about the fact that I'd have to walk all the way.

"At walking speed about a four-hour walk. But we're not doing that, of course."

I raised an eyebrow. "How are we going to get there? We're in the middle of nowhere."

I was hoping I didn't have to get on top of a flying horse again, but before I could inquire a bat flew past me and startled me. I looked around for Rosabella, didn't see her and realized that she had transformed again.

"And how are we supposed to … ?"

"You're going to piggyback ride," answered Bluebell. I thought she was joking for a second, but she looked dead serious. I just looked at her as if she was making an insensitive joke.

"I'm serious," Bluebell said and couldn't help but laugh. "Come on."

Bluebell turned her back towards me and made a hand gesture.

"I'm not – no!"

Bluebell turned back to me. "Stubborn, aren't you? I promise it'll be fine."

I just shook my head lightly. Rosabella the bat, meanwhile was flying around us in circles.

Bluebell finally sighed and started walking up to me, and I backed away cautiously. Bluebell then picked me up, effortlessly and swung me over her shoulder.

I let out a small yelp. "Okay, okay, fine! Will you put me down?"

So, she did. I turned to face her back and she squatted down a bit.

"Uhm," I said, awkwardly touching Bluebell's shoulder, trying to figure out how on earth to do this without breaking her bony back.

"Just jump."

"But … "

"Junie," Bluebell said in as exasperated tone, "just jump, please."

I sighed, braced myself and jumped awkwardly onto Bluebell's back. Having only one good leg made me land on her pretty hard. She grabbed my legs, being careful with my hurt leg, threw me up a little bit to position me better and started walking. I put my arms around Bluebell's neck. Having a person on her back didn't seem to bother her or slow her down one bit.

"Is this okay?" she asked.

"Yes, thank you," I answered, surprised that she was still standing, let alone walking.

Rosabella the bat was now flying next to us.

"Okay, then hold on tightly. We're gonna run."

Before I could say anything or ask another nervous question, Bluebell started running faster than I had ever seen anyone run. I tightened my grip around her neck as the wind hit my face, arms, one of which still had a fresh wound and my hair. I squinted my eyes and held my breath. It took about a minute for me to realize that Bluebell was not going to slow down. I attempted to open my eyes, seeing through the wind that was slapping me in the face. Rosabella the bat made an appearance beside us from time to time. I saw the woodlands racing by us, too fast and too dark to really take good notice of anything. The outlines of trees flew by. Paths flew by. We ran past a river, jumped some rocks and ran over and down some hills. The moonlight was the only way for me to see the shadowy outlines of all that passed by.

"You still all right there?" asked Bluebell effortlessly, after a while.

"Yes," I breathed. "You?"

"Yes! We're almost there, it's just on the other side of that cave."

I looked ahead and was just in time to notice the entrance of a cave before the last bit of light disappeared and we were inside; but just as quickly as we went in, we were outside again, and Bluebell started to slow down.

It was odd to be on her back for other reasons than just the obvious ones. It was odd because we had never had physical contact for this long. Bluebell usually had tried her best not to shy away from normal human contact like hugs and sitting close to me in general, but she had always struggled with that. Come to think of it, I thought, Bluebell had been acting a bit differently since I had been bitten. It seemed that she had dared to sit closer to me, seemed a little less nervous, less distant and overall more … relaxed. My thought process was interrupted as Bluebell started walking and then stood still, giving me the chance to slide off her.

I stood back on my good leg and found a tree to lean against and Rosabella (in human form) came walking up from behind me. She was looking at something.

I followed her gaze and noticed that ahead of us was a small cabin. We had reached what looked like a small ghost town. There were several cabins, or small houses, but they all seemed deserted. None of them had any lights on and most of them had their windows broken. There was no light anywhere, only the shining of the moon.

"What is this place?"

"It's called Larua," explained Bluebell. "People think it's a haunted place but it's not," she added when she saw my frown. "This is where Ubel resides with his new-borns. This is where I used to live a long time ago."

Larua seemed deserted. There didn't seem to be any sign of life anywhere. It was weird to see what was supposed to be a town without any stores, facilities, cars or anything people used daily. There was no sign of life anywhere at all. It was deserted.

"Is it … supposed to be this quiet?" I asked.

"No," answered Bluebell while suspiciously looking around. "It isn't crowded or anything but there's always someone here … but let's not forget that Ubel set out to have everyone killed."

Bluebell started walking forward, up to the little battered cabin and looked through one of the broken windows.

"No one's here," said Bluebell, unsurprised. "Let's check out Ubel's place first."

We started to walk around the deserted village, Rosabella kindly holding me up. We walked along several abandoned, empty streets and stopped in front of a cabin that stood on its own at the end of one particularly long street. It was an eerie place, there was no sound anywhere and there was a faint fog hovering in the air. Bluebell peeked through the windows, some intact and some broken, then eventually opened a squeaky door and went inside for a moment. After a minute or so, she came back to Rosabella and me.

"Empty. So, listen ... when I talked to Ellison and Etana they said that Endora had been acting strangely for months. She hadn't been around a lot ... At first they weren't worried because she seemed to be fine but then she started to act weirdly as time went by. She was stressed about something, always looking over her shoulder. Eventually, she told them she was going away for a while and that if anything happened they should look for a chest somewhere in Ubel's residence."

"A chest?" asked Rosabella. "She must have been planning something for a while. I wonder where she went, if she was away from home so much."

Bluebell nodded. "Let's uhm, look for a chest, I guess. The coast should be clear. If Ubel ran off, then nobody else should be around either."

And so, we went inside what was supposed to be Ubel's house. It was just a cabin and it looked ancient, just like the rest, as if there hadn't been anyone living in the town for centuries.

I had to take out the flashlight to see. The wallpaper was peeling and there was no light anywhere, not even light bulbs or any sort of lamps. There was an extreme build-up of dust and there were cobwebs everywhere. I made the mistake of shining my torch down onto the ground and my eyes fell on a set of bones which were unmistakably human. I tried my best to suppress my gagging reflexes. Among all the filth and the skeleton on the floor there were some ancient looking chairs standing around, and a blackened fireplace, which told me we had to be standing in what was once a living room. I was far from completing my examination when I heard Rosabella yell from a different room.

Bluebell and I came to her from different directions. She was standing next to a wooden chest in the corner of an empty room. It looked old but was still too modern for the small house it was standing in. Rosabella backed away as Bluebell went closer to the chest and left her to deal with it.

"Well, here goes nothing," she said with a sigh, and attempted to open it. To everyone's surprise, it opened right away – it wasn't locked. Bluebell opened the lid and before Rosabella and I could have a look she let it fall shut again and backed away with a gasp. She put her hand to her head to compose herself and went silent.

"What is it?" asked Rosabella.

"It's … It's a kid. Dead," answered Bluebell in shock.

I couldn't help but frown.

"A vampire child. It's like the worst crime a vampire can commit," explained Bluebell.

"So, they murdered them? Why? And why is that so bad?"

So killing and torturing adults was okay and encouraged, but hurting children was considered immoral? I felt slightly offended by the hypocrisy of it all.

"Because they are the epitome of immortality," explained Bluebell impatiently. "They are forever children. They don't age. They never even reach adulthood. Vampire children are treated like royals among vampires."

"So there's a murdered vampire child in that chest?" I asked, my arms now crossed. "Why?"

Rosabella stepped forward. "Well, let's look."

Bluebell nodded hesitantly and opened the chest again. She and Rosabella looked inside while I shone the flashlight and had a look as well. Inside was indeed a dead child, a dead vampire child. It was a small boy, who had the physique of a child of approximately eight years old. This wasn't a deceased child who had been prepped to look peaceful and serene in his coffin. This child had been murdered.

I never asked for confirmation, but it seemed to me that the way vampires killed each other was through decapitation. Endora, Fallax and Ignacia had all been decapitated when I saw them after they had died.

This little boy also had a severed head, and it was the most disturbing death I had seen so far. Even though this kid was a vampire and lived a different life than any human child, it was still a child, and he still had a look of innocence. I stared at the child's copper locks for a moment, wondering if it was a coincidence that they looked so much like Bluebell's.

Bluebell moved forward with a frown on her face and reached out to towards the gap between his severed head and his torso. She put her hand down his T-shirt a little bit and found a necklace. She pulled the necklace out and had a look of pure disgust on her face as she brought towards her a small silver vessel. It looked like the vessel was an assault to her hand.

She unscrewed the top and before she even moved it closer to her nose as I was expecting her to do, the look of disgust she had on her face turned into one of fury.

"What is it?" asked Rosabella.

Bluebell just screwed the top back on, put it back in the chest and remained silent for a moment.

"It's blood," she mumbled eventually. "It's Oliver's."

"What?" I asked before Rosabella could, "but ... what? How?"

"I don't know!" she said aggressively. "I have no fucking clue! But look at this kid for crying out loud! Look at his hair and that fucking olive T-shirt! And they have his blood!"

"Blue ..."

"He is alive, and they are going to kill him," she snarled. "Once I get my fucking hands on them they ..."

"Bluebell, do you think ... They turned him back?" interrupted Rosabella.

"Probably! I don't know!" Bluebell barked, looking as if she was about to lose it. "I'm seeing just as much as you two, I'm not ..."

"Bluebell!" an unfamiliar but cheerful voice interrupted her.

Instinctively we all turned our heads towards the door, with me pointing the flashlight. A slim, black-haired man who was unmistakably also a vampire came walking towards us with a big smile on his pale face. His long raven hair fell slightly over his face, and he was dressed all in black with platform boots, making him look even taller than he was.

"Hey," said Bluebell, looking pleasantly surprised for once.

He walked up to us, and they hugged.

"What are you doing here?" asked Bluebell.

"I found out that Ubel left, so I came to see what was going on! What are you doing here?"

"Long story ..."

"I have the time," he said with a friendly smile, "but let me introduce myself first."

He turned towards Rosabella and me.

"Rosa," he said as he gave her a friendly nod. Rosabella did not seem like the type to hug people. I figured this guy had the same idea. He then stuck out his hand to me.

"I'm Onyx, nice to meet you," he said and smiled, exposing his fangs, squinting a bit at the light coming from my flashlight, which I quickly pointed down.

I shook his cold hand. "I'm Junie, nice to meet you too."

I didn't know much about Onyx, but I had heard his name before when Bluebell was talking to him on the phone. She had mentioned that Onyx absolutely hated Ubel. It wasn't hard to hate Ubel; but I wondered why Onyx hated him so much that it was worth specifically mentioning.

"Junie ..." he said as he raised his trimmed eyebrows in surprise, "but ... you're not human. Who bit you?"

"We don't know," said Bluebell. "Somebody knocked her and Rosabella out with chloroform when I was away. She woke up bitten."

"Chloroform ..." Onyx mused, "that's not something you hear every day."

"No," said Bluebell in agreement.

Onyx's attention quickly returned to the story Bluebell hadn't told him yet.

"So, what happened? Why are you here?" he said as he put an arm around her.

"Well, you know about the fight."

Onyx looked at her curiously, as much as was possible with plain white eyes, and nodded.

"Uhm ...," she started, "we found out that Endora was coming to tell me about my brother."

"You have a brother?" Onyx asked, trying to connect the dots.

"Well, I had a brother ... I thought he was dead."

"But he's not? So now you're searching for him?"

"Yes."

"Okay so ... you think Ubel had Endora killed then, is that why you're here?"

Bluebell nodded.

"And what about the fight?"

"Well, that's the thing ... They all started killing each other. They had human hearts. And so did Endora." She added, "They were given a cure."

"Really?" said Onyx, and his entire tone changed. "A cure?"

"Yes," said Bluebell while casting him a look as if to keep him on the topic. "It must have been given to them. We think Ubel set out to kill all of them to ensure there'd be no more traitors."

"My, my ..." said Onyx, putting his hand to his face, ruminating. "So Endora was about to spill some secrets ..."

Bluebell nodded, still in Onyx's embrace. The sight of Bluebell being so physically close with someone seemed weird to me. She didn't seem to mind it, however.

"Yeah ... I talked to the twins about Endora to see if they knew anything. They said she'd been acting oddly for a while; going away for long periods of time, being secretive and distant.

144

She eventually told them that she was going to go away and that if something happened they should look for a chest. So, we came here to look for a chest and for Devlin and Ubel, but clearly they're not here."

They both looked at the chest in front of them. Onyx took his arm from around Bluebell's shoulder and went to open it.

"Oh dear," he said in a sympathetic voice. "This must be what she saw?"

Bluebell shrugged. Onyx's eyes fastened onto the necklace that was now plain to see.

"What's in there?" he asked.

"It's my brother's blood," said Bluebell coldly.

"Very strange indeed ..." he muttered, then turning back to Bluebell, he said, "Why don't I help you?"

Bluebell gave him a sceptical look. Then her expression changed.

"*Oh,*" she said.

Onyx gave her a small smile that didn't look sincere but rather, tortured.

"There's no time to waste," said Onyx, gathering himself again. Somehow his voice sounded both mysterious and amused every time he spoke, as if he was on a treasure hunt or solving some type of puzzle. "Your brother is clearly alive, isn't he? And somehow he is human. I think the dead child is a clear warning that he is in danger."

Bluebell beamed at him. At least now she had someone with her who was on the same wavelength.

"But where could he be?" she then asked.

"Hm ..." Onyx went to open the chest again and scanned the body of the child.

Suddenly, his hand moved towards the boy's already slightly opened mouth and parted his lips. Mortified at what he was doing, I froze and watched. So did the others. He bowed to look inside the child's mouth and with a blank expression started to pull something out of it. It was a leaf. He stood back and held the leaf out in front of him while we all curiously watched. I shined my light on it and could make the number one hundred and seventy-one.

"You're a genius," said Bluebell excitedly.

"Always playing games, that asshole," Onyx sighed.

"What's your connection to him? Did Ubel bite you too?" I asked curiously.

Onyx nodded. "Yeah," he said with a defeated voice. "It kind of got in the way of my future plans. I've been keeping track of them to make sure they don't come for my wife."

His wife. I hadn't thought yet about vampires having relationships. Imagine if one day you're in a happy, normal, human relationship and the next day you or your spouse are immortal with a thirst for blood … Your blood.

"Oh yeah!" exclaimed Bluebell a little too excited. Her mood seemed to have improved a little now that there was a clue. "Onyx's wife is a werewolf too! She's in one of the Noctiluca packs! You should talk to her!"

Onyx raised an eyebrow at me. "You don't have a pack yet? I'm sure my wife would be happy to raise you. I'll introduce you two later."

I stared at them dumbfounded. When Onyx said he was making sure that they didn't come for his wife I figured she had to be human. Bluebell couldn't help but laugh at the expression on my face as I was trying to process everything.

"You know what," she said with a smile, and it was nice to see her laugh after this whole situation, "let's get together with her later and you can ask her everything you want. First we've got to figure out what on earth this number means … and give this poor boy the ceremony he deserves."

"We should search him some more," said Onyx. Bluebell hesitantly nodded at him. "I'll do it," Onyx said. "Why don't you all go outside and think about that number?"

He handed the leaf to Bluebell, turned back to the kid and the rest of us went outside. We sat down against the frail outside of the cabin. Bluebell was examining the leaf. I shined the light on it and joined her. Rosabella was looking with me, making use of the bits of light I was providing.

"One hundred and seventy-one …" mumbled Rosabella. "Maybe it's a house number, or some sort of building?"

"Maybe," said Bluebell doubtingly, "or some type of coordinates."

She turned the leaf over but there was nothing there, so she turned it back.

"He'd better still be alive," she grunted eventually.

"He has to be, right? How else would they have gotten the blood?" I asked, in an attempt to sound consoling.

At that moment, Onyx walked out of the cabin. He handed the necklace with the vessel over to Bluebell, with a pained expression, who put it in her pocket while pulling a similar pained expression.

Onyx then held out his other hand in which he was holding a piece of paper. Bluebell seized it and looked at it. I shone the flashlight on it. It had one simple quote, or rather, one simple pun: 'Live, Laugh, Clove.'

"Live, laugh, clove?" said Bluebell, clearly not amused. "Do you know what this means?"

Onyx shook his head. Rosabella did the same when she looked at her.

"It's from that shop in town," I answered, slightly confused, "that little herb shop. They specialize in garlic." Bluebell and Onyx instantly had a look of disgust on their faces. "What?" I asked.

"Vampires hate garlic," Bluebell said.

"Oh," I said, surprised – really; garlic of all things? "Do you think he is being held … in a garlic shop?"

"That's not so bad if he's human," thought Bluebell aloud, "but it is bad for us."

"What if they turned him back?" asked Onyx.

"Can you re-turn a vampire after he's been cured?" asked Rosabella.

"I don't see why not," answered Onyx.

"But do you really think they would keep him right here, in town?" asked Bluebell. "In a store that people go past every day?"

"I don't know, Bluebell. All of this is sketchy and just plain weird if you ask me," sighed Onyx, "but it's worth looking into."

"Well, let's go," said Bluebell as she started getting up. "No time to waste, right?"

"Agreed," said Onyx, "you go on ahead, I'll fetch Amaeka and we'll both help you."

Bluebell nodded and Rosabella helped me get up as we prepared to go to the town centre.

Chapter Twenty

Rosabella had transformed into a bat again and I was back on Bluebell's back as we raced towards the town centre. I couldn't see much but I decided I trusted Bluebell enough to feel safe. This running might have been fun during the day, I thought to myself, when I could see, but right now this felt just like sitting in a car with someone who wasn't fit to drive.

Eventually, we stopped somewhere on a hill opposite where we had just come from and we could see the houses and lit streets of Cunabula. Even though we were standing still, Bluebell kept me on her back as if I were as light as a feather. Rosabella the bat was now hanging upside down from a tree.

"We're just waiting for Onyx and Amaeka," Bluebell said to me, while gazing down at the town beneath us. "You said you know where it is, can you lead the way?"

"Sure," I answered, I had visited the small garlic-oriented shop before.

Bluebell loosened her grip on my legs to let me get off her back and she put her arm around me for support.

"How do you feel?" I asked.

She was still gazing in the distance. "I don't know … I don't feel much. I don't know what to expect," she said irritably. "I'm trying to just keep my head in the game for now."

After a few minutes of waiting, we heard rushing footsteps coming towards us and eventually saw Onyx and his wife emerging from the woods. He was carrying her just like Bluebell carried me and let her down once they reached us. Standing next to Onyx in his platform boots, she was just slightly shorter than him. She was a bald woman with dark eyes, and she was tall and slim just like her husband. She had beautifully drawn eyebrows with a slash in her left eyebrow. She went to hug Bluebell just like Onyx had done, nodded the same way at Rosabella the bat who was still hanging upside down in the tree and then also stuck out her hand for me to shake.

"Amaeka," she said, and smiled warmly. It was nice to see someone new who had colour in their eyes for once.

"Junie," I said as I shook her hand and smiled back, glad that her hand felt warm.

Onyx smiled too and put his arm on his wife's back. They made quite a couple, I thought. Amaeka was dressed less alternatively but also wore all black and simply looked like a badass woman.

"What's the plan?" asked Amaeka.

"We run to the edge of the forest and then we walk to the garlic store. Junie knows where it is. There isn't a plan. We just have to get inside," answered Bluebell.

Amaeka and Onyx both nodded, then she jumped up on Onyx's back again without warning and Bluebell gestured at me to do the same.

We set off again with Rosabella flying next to us. At the edge of the forest, Bluebell went to retrieve her contacts from the backpack I had with me and put them in. She instantly looked more alive. She gave Onyx another pair and he reluctantly put them in too. Then she got out a wireless drill like machine and without any type of care, started going at her fangs with it. They looked like normal human teeth a moment later and she handed the device to Onyx who started doing the same, more cautiously and awkwardly and after a moment his seemed normal too. Rosabella had turned back into her woman form again. Bluebell checked all our appearances and when she approved, we started walking into Cunabula.

Since it was the middle of the night, there wasn't really anyone out. Here and there were bars where people were partying and some lights in the houses were on. A car raced by every so often but no one was walking around. I led the way towards the town centre with Bluebell supporting me and when we came close, I noticed that something was not right. It was getting crowded and we started seeing blue lights. We heard people talking, and eventually, in the street where the garlic store was located, we saw several police cars parked right in front of where we had to be. A crowd of people had gathered.

"Shit!" hissed Bluebell.

I bent over and quickly tore Rosabella's DIY solution off my leg that had kept it stable this far. It didn't feel good, but I could hardly walk over there looking like a child had played doctor on my leg. It was almost a given that my mother was at the scene, after all.

"What do we do?" asked Rosabella. "What do we say?"

I noticed that Onyx was starting to look uncomfortable, Amaeka tried to comfort him.

"We were walking Junie home and happened to notice the commotion so we went to look. Remember, we're all human," said Bluebell as we walked to the scene.

Bluebell wasted no time and took me to the front of the crowd, bulldozing through as if the other people weren't there.

"Ms Marcelin!" exclaimed Bluebell.

"Bluebell! *Junie!*" My mother said as she rushed over to us. "You're back!"

She swung her arms around me and hugged me tight and gave Bluebell an appropriate hug after me.

"Why are you two out here at this time? It's not safe!"

"Don't worry, a couple of our friends are with us! We were just walking Junie home when we noticed that something was going on," Bluebell explained. "What exactly *is* going on?"

My mother looked at us with eyes that told us she would rather not explain. She pulled up the police tape and pulled us inside the officer filled scene, away from the crowd. Rosabella, Onyx and Amaeka were now standing in front of the police tape where we had been standing, with Onyx looking more and more uneasy by the second.

"There is someone inside that store," she said softly, "but … he is dangerous. We have a body on the other side of the store. He threw the other person out of the window. He doesn't want to come out. We already had to fire shots, but unfortunately, he seems unaffected. We don't know what to do. If bullets don't work we can't go in."

Bluebell's expression turned cold. "Ms Marcelin, may I ask what this person looks like?" she asked cautiously. We heard another siren coming closer and some sort of vehicle approaching.

"Please just call me Esther, dear," my mother said quickly before answering. "It's a white male. Tall, slightly muscular, with red hair; I'm guessing about twenty-five years old. The weird thing is that his eyes are white, and so were the eyes of the person who died. Oh, speaking of that, the body exactly matches the description you ..."

Bluebell was already gone. She was running the distance towards the entrance, with appropriate human speed, but still running.

"STOP!" yelled another officer. "HEY! DON'T MOVE!"

Bluebell didn't stop. A warning shot was fired but she kept running and when she reached the entrance after pushing some officers aside, she kicked in the door and disappeared into the dark store. I couldn't see what was going on. All the police officers stood frozen to the spot and my mother was looking horrified, her hands in front of her mouth. Several gasps could be heard from the crowd as Bluebell went inside and everyone seemed to be waiting anxiously to see what would happen. I looked at the crowd and saw that Rosabella wasn't there anymore. I looked back at the entrance but I didn't see her there either. Onyx and Amaeka came running towards the entrance, having sneaked under the police tape, ignoring the commotion.

Several officers started yelling at them too, but neither of them stopped.

"Sorry, Mum, I have to," I mumbled, before I rushed into the store as fast as I could, grimacing from the pain in my leg. More yelling came from the officers.

They were fed up with everyone going in, but they didn't try to stop me. I heard my mother screaming; "DON'T YOU DARE, THAT IS MY DAUGHTER!"

I went inside through the broken door and my eyes fell on the silhouette of Bluebell pinning someone to the ground. I quickly looked for a light switch and flipped it.

Bluebell, who was stronger than I thought possible, was currently struggling to push someone down on the ground and she had to be assisted, so she wouldn't be overpowered. Bluebell was face down on top of this person while Amaeka and Rosabella were each holding an arm down, being smacked away every few seconds, and Onyx was pushing down on the person's legs, with more success. I walked over to get a better look.

Underneath Bluebell was a man who indeed looked about twenty-five years old, with ginger, messy hair, very similar to Bluebell's. He was tall, lean and his eyes were white as snow. He was fighting with all his power to get away from the people on top of him. I noticed that his fangs were broken.

They weren't long, but they weren't human-like either, and it looked like he had somehow bitten down on a brick and shattered his teeth. His skin was as white as snow, just like Bluebell's, except that he had deep wounds all over him. They looked like bullet wounds.

"Come on, just a few more," said Bluebell as she did her best to keep him still. She leaned over and pushed her fingers into one of his wounds, extracting a bullet. I flinched at the sight.

She hissed as she touched it, the same pained expression as when she had touched the necklace with the vessel, and quickly threw it away across the room. I noticed several others lying around as well; this wasn't the first one she had removed. But the removal of one more bullet did not calm him down one bit. She moved on to the next wound.

"Why are the police here?" asked Onyx, while struggling to hold him down.

"He killed someone," I answered while it only just started sinking in as Onyx asked the question. I scanned the store and my eyes fell on the broken window in the back.

I hopped over to it and looked outside. There was another crowd being held back by police tape and officers, and other police members were taking tools out of a van.

In front of the van, which had been parked so the bystanders couldn't see – was a body. And I didn't have to look twice to see who it was.

"Devlin," I said, shocked.

"He killed Devlin?" asked Onyx right before he got kicked hard in the stomach and whimpered.

The officers were now covering up Devlin's body; and severed head.

No one there seemed to notice what was going on inside the store. I turned back to the others and noticed that on the side of the store we had come from, people were looking. A bunch of officers were keeping a close eye on what was going on inside, coming closer now, and several of them had their guns drawn.

"We have to get him out of here," I said.

Bluebell threw yet another bullet away with a pained expression on her face. As she opened her mouth to answer, she suddenly got bitten in the shoulder, and I saw a whole chunk of her snow-white flesh being torn off. She shrieked. "Motherfucker," she groaned, trying to compose herself. "I think there's only, ..." she paused to whimper, "one more bullet left. If I can just get that one out ..."

But before she could finish a shot was fired and a bullet came flying in from a broken window. Onyx flew into the air and jumped-up in the path of the bullet. It hit him ... but then the bullet bounced right off him. It then occurred to me that the police bullets weren't going to seriously injure either Bluebell or Onyx, or ...

"So, is this your brother?" I asked Bluebell.

"Yes, it's him," she said while still struggling to hold him still and trying to penetrate the last wound that still had a bullet in it with her fingers.

"Okay, good," I said, "but we have to leave. They are shooting, if they hit Amaeka or Rosabella or me ..."

"Don't worry about it," said Onyx as he cheekily walked from cop to cop, as if daring them to shoot. "They are only aiming for Oliver and I can catch any bullet they fire. Cops don't shoot with silver."

"Get the legs, Junie," said Bluebell in response, wanting me to take over what Onyx had been doing.

I nodded and grabbed hold of Oliver's legs, but it was a losing game. It was as if he was kicking something with the weight of a balloon instead of the grip of a person. I got kicked away only seconds after and was shoved backwards by the force. I hastily limped back.

I heard more shots being fired but from the corner of my eye I saw Onyx moving faster than the speed of light to catch every single one of them.

"We are *trying* to get this man to calm down here," said Onyx to the shooters. "Would you please just let us do that for a second?!"

"Got it!" said Bluebell as she threw away the last bullet. It then dawned on me that Oliver must have been in so much pain because unlike the police bullets, like Onyx had mentioned, the bullets he had been shot with were silver. Silver is supposed to hurt vampires, say all the myths. It must be true...

But even with all the bullets removed, Oliver did not calm down. He was not screaming or making much noise at all, other than the slamming of his limbs on the wooden floor of the store, shattering it, and as he struggled against the people trying to hold him down, but he was whimpering and softly moaning in agony.

"He's not calming down," said Bluebell with increasing panic in her voice. "There must be something else wrong."

"Garlic," said Amaeka suddenly, a look of urgency on her face. "It must be garlic!"

"You're right," said Bluebell, her voice softening. "Uhm, okay, let's see ..." She looked around the room, as much as she could, with the flailing man underneath her.

Oliver hit Rosabella with so much force that she groaned. That would surely take it's toll later on. It didn't seem to distract Bluebell.

"Rosa, I need you to go outside and talk to those officers, please. Tell them to please stay put. Amaeka, I need you to distract the officers on the other side. We can't have them peeking in. Onyx, you and I will keep him down and open his stomach. Junie, I need you to get the garlic out."

"I need to *what?* You're going to open his stomach?!" I asked, mortified.

"We need to get it out. It's the only way."

Amaeka and Rosabella quickly went to the officers with their hands up to show them that no harm was intended and went outside to talk to them.

"Let's move him over there," said Bluebell as she jerked her head in the direction of the counter.

Onyx rushed over, there were no more bullets flying about, at least for now and he took Oliver's legs from me. Bluebell got off Oliver to grab his arms. As soon as she got off him Oliver started flailing even worse, trying to bite. I could see his whole body convulsing as if it were beyond his control. With difficulty, they managed to move Oliver behind the small counter, so they were out of sight from the crowd and hidden from the windows and the onlookers. Onyx and Bluebell put their full body weight on Oliver's limbs in a desperate attempt to keep him still. As time ticked by, Oliver's whimpers started to get more desperate. He almost sounded like he was crying. Bluebell had an expression on her face that was nearly as pain- ful as his. At the same time, I could hear yelling from outside and I assumed that it had to be the officers getting impatient, increasingly worried for everyone's safety. Perhaps they were preparing to come in.

"Ready, Junie?" asked Bluebell.

"What do I do?" I asked anxiously.

"We're gonna open him up and you have to get the garlic out. I know it's gross, I'm sorry you have to do this, but please ..." she looked at me with a pleading look.

"Yes, of course," I said reassuringly, "but how? How do I ...?"

"All that there's going to be in there is blood," explained Onyx, "old blood. It's going to be dark, some of it is going to be dried up. You're going to think it's gross, but you'll have to look for pieces of garlic in the blood."

I felt my stomach turn. I did not want to do this for the life of me.

"Okay," I said as I braced myself, and threw myself down in a sitting position next to Oliver. Bluebell put her knees on Oliver's arms and used her arms to grab hold of Oliver's head – he had already started trying to bite me the second I sat down.

"I'll do it," said Onyx, looking at Bluebell.

"Thank you," she said, so soft it was almost inaudible.

"Remember Junie, you have to work quickly, it's going to start healing right away."

I nodded at Onyx, cast a quick look at the bullet wounds on Oliver that were indeed already looking more like old wounds – not that they had bled to begin with.

Onyx locked eyes with both Bluebell and I before pulling up Oliver's shirt, and opened his mouth wider than I had ever seen anybody open their mouth, besides maybe a snake on TV, and sunk his teeth into Oliver's stomach. The screech he let out sent shivers down my spine to the point where I felt my body involuntarily freeze. Onyx then rose again with a huge chunk of Oliver's flesh in his mouth and spat it out on the floor. He went in again, ignoring Oliver's screaming and took out another chunk. He kept doing this until there was an actual hole in Oliver's stomach, wide and deep enough for both my hands to fit in and the first blood started to come out. A thick, dense goo of blood started to flow out of him as if it were a morbid type of ketchup. Despite it moving so slow, it started flowing out in every direction; down his sides, onto his chest, onto his pelvis and all around him on the floor. There was a lot of it. It was more blood than I had ever seen and the fact that this was voluntarily in someone's stomach made me want to gag. The metallic smell was assaulting my nose. I tried to ignore the thought that this blood had to have come from someone, several people, rather.

"Now, Junie!" snapped Bluebell.

I took a deep breath, which I instantly regretted, leaned over Oliver and tried not to throw up as I put my hand inside the bloody hole. The blood felt more liquid than it looked. I started feeling around, ignoring the chunks of clotted, sometimes semi-dried blood I could feel and after a few seconds I felt something hard and round. I took it out and saw that it was a whole garlic bulb, horrifyingly stained black and red. I wondered if I had ever been this nauseous before.

"Yes," said Bluebell relieved. "Well done, Junie!" Underneath her, however, Oliver was still whimpering, barely moving anymore. "It's almost over, Oli," said Bluebell lovingly as she stroked his hair.

I fished around some more, trying not to breathe more than I had to, and eventually took out two more solid bulbs of garlic. I was feeling lightheaded at that point but I was impressed with myself for still being okay. At last, focusing with all my might, I found a fourth and last bulb and the second I took it out, Oliver fell silent and stopped moving altogether. I could have sworn at that moment that the hole in his stomach had already shrunk a little bit.

"It's over!" said Bluebell. "They're all out, Oli!"

Oliver seemed to be coming out of a trance and he started looking around. Bluebell and Onyx got off him and sat down on the floor beside him. Bluebell was staring at him as if she just found a treasure and couldn't take her eyes off him for one second. Onyx was observing him curiously. Fully aware that I was ruining the moment, I couldn't hold it back anymore and I quickly got up, threw myself over the counter and vomited. It seemed at that moment that we all snapped back to reality and noticed the loud yelling coming from outside. I could hear Rosabella and Amaeka's voices loudly trying to reason with raised, angry voices, but it sounded like they were both losing their arguments. I wiped my mouth and looked out the window and saw once again that there were several guns pointed at us inside. I quickly got back behind the counter. The yelling got louder. Oliver was starting to look scared and backed away.

"It's okay, Oli," whispered Bluebell. Oliver did not seem to think so.

"We have to go, Bluebell," said Onyx as he looked toward one of the windows. "They're coming in."

She nodded in understanding. "We have to create some sort of diversion so we can sneak him out through the back ... You must take him," she said decidedly to Onyx. "Rosa can take you to my bunker. I'll go to through the front with Amaeka and Junie and say he escaped or something. We'll come up with something."

Onyx nodded. Suddenly Bluebell was yelling, which startled Oliver even more. "ROSA! DISTRACTION AT THE FRONT! NOW!"

I didn't even have time to register what she had just said because barely a second later I could hear screaming outside, coming from the back of the store, and then the screaming moving to the front of the store, like a wave. I heard the clapping of what sounded like huge wings and a deafening, beast like roar the likes of which I'd never heard before. Then I heard a loud bang of something hitting the ground and I felt like I could feel the ground shake at that moment. Bluebell quickly stood up and looked through the back window.

"Clear!" she said, which was meant for Onyx, who instantly grabbed Oliver, who was looking more horrified and confused by the second, by his arm and started running towards the broken back window. He jumped out, quickly pulled Oliver through the broken glass and ran off into the night.

Bluebell reached out her hand to help me get up. I took it, stood up and looked through the windows in the front ... And saw what seemed to be the torso of a ginormous, fire red,

scaly creature. It was stomping around and still roaring. Was it ... A dragon?

"ROSA! BUNKER! GO!"

Immediately, the creature let out another deafening roar, followed by even more terrified screams from the people outside. I heard a few shots being fired but it didn't seem to have any effect on the situation and the creature flew up into the air, the loud sound of huge wings clapping in the sky went over us and then started to slowly fade into the distance, leaving with one last roar. I saw the mortified looks of the people outside.

Bluebell took me by the arm and led us outside through the door she had previously kicked down; where we saw Amaeka standing tall and proud among the police officers. We walked up to her, but she winked and started walking away before we got there.

"Junie!" My mother rushed forward and once again gave me a bone-cracking hug. "Oh, and Bluebell, I'm so glad you two are all right!"

"He got away, Ms ... Esther," Bluebell corrected herself. "He left. Our friends went after him but who knows if they'll catch up with him ..."

"*Why on earth* did you run in to begin with?! You should know better!"

"I guess I just wanted to help," said Bluebell in a fake defeated voice.

My mother didn't seem to buy it, but she also did not seem in the mood to argue.

"Why don't you two go home? I'll ask someone to give you a ride," she said, and then looked at my leg that was floating just above the ground. "After we get someone to look at your leg."

"I think I'll just get a taxi, but thank you," Bluebell said politely. My mother nodded.

"Aren't you coming home then, Mum?" I asked.

"No, no ... We have ... a lot of work to do at the station."

"Shit!" cursed Bluebell softly to me after my mother went to talk to some of the paramedics on site. "Devlin's body. We can't leave it there."

But at that very moment, a panicked officer came running and yelled something about the body being gone.

"That thing! It must've taken it!"

"Come on, now, you really believe that?" answered another sceptical officer.

"Come look if you don't believe me, Paul! Everything is burnt and the body is gone! I tell you, that thing did it!"

I saw Bluebell's lips curl up into a smile, but she quickly changed her expression back when my mother came walking back.

"Come, Junie," she said and walked off to one of the vans and we followed her.

"So, dragons, huh?" I asked Bluebell softly.

"Tip of the iceberg, June," she said and couldn't suppress her sneaky smile any longer.

Chapter Twenty-One

Winds of Change

I was sitting on the couch with my sleepy father after having taken a quick but thorough shower to get rid of all the blood, the dirt and the filth of not having showered in days and having lived in a filthy underground bunker. I did have to wear long sleeves to hide the bite marks. We sat watching the breaking news story on what had happened. They showed footage of the broken window of the store, the sheets on top of where Devlin's body had lain, the police tape, and they interviewed some officers.

They didn't mention anything about a body that had disappeared, or a gigantic dragon and the fire it had breathed. I decided not to tell my father either – I left that to my mother who didn't have ridiculous sounding truths to hide. My dad sighed as the announcement was over and turned the TV off.

"What has come of this town?" he said mournfully.

"I don't know, Dad," I said.

"And what has gotten into you, going inside like that? You broke your leg for crying out loud!"

"I went in to help Bluebell, I didn't want her to be in there by herself."

"Is it a coincidence that every time you get into trouble it's with that girl? I don't mean to question your choice in friends, dear, but this is not the first time."

I didn't take offence because he made a very good point. If only he knew that Bluebell was indeed the reason; and if only he knew exactly why that was.

"It is a coincidence. She just wanted to help," I told him.

He let out a soft sigh but accepted my answer and nodded. "Well, I'm happy you're back but I'd like you not to go outside alone anymore. Especially not at night."

I nodded. "You be careful too, Dad."

We smiled faintly at each other.

"Are there any updates on the case? What happened while I was away?"

He looked away. "Three more people were killed, found in the same state as the others. Whoever did it didn't bother to hide them, two of them were found dead in their own homes and one on the street. They still have no new leads."

I looked away. So, Ubel and Devlin had killed three more people. Bluebell wouldn't leave them like that, and I hadn't heard yet of any other vampires hunting in town.

"Maybe they'll figure some of it out tonight," he continued. "If this guy killed someone in that store he might've had something to do with the others, don't you think?"

"Maybe," I said, pretending to agree at first, but then I wondered if it *could* have been Oliver. He was in town, and he didn't seem all there. Maybe he didn't care about leaving a trail. Or what about Onyx?

"Your mother and I think we should move," my father said suddenly.

I looked up in surprise. "Move? Really? You've lived here for decades."

"It's not safe anymore, Junie," he answered with a pained expression on his face. "We'd like you to come with us. Please, consider."

"I will, thank you," I said and smiled at him. I got up and stretched. "I'm going to sleep now, see you tomorrow."

I looked at the clock and noticed that six a.m. was nearing.

"Goodnight, sweetheart."

"Goodnight, Dad."

I went upstairs and dropped onto my bed. It felt like the mattress was hugging my every bone and muscle. I fell asleep before I could put the blanket over myself.

The next day I woke up with my body feeling sore and slightly feverish again, or still? Maybe I had been so pumped with adrenaline I didn't feel myself still recovering from being bitten. I opened my eyes, directly got hit with sunlight and realized that I must've slept for a long time.

I checked my phone and saw that it was three in the afternoon. I also saw that I had a missed call from Bluebell from a few hours earlier.

Then a text that said, 'Just wanted to check on you. Everything is OK here. Call me. X'

I sat up straight and dialled her number.

"Good morning," joked Bluebell.

"G-good morning," I said while trying to supress a yawn. "What's up?"

"Well, we all spent the night here, except for Amaeka because she had to go home to sleep. Rosa slept in the bunker and we spent most of the night trying to break through to Oliver. He is … Not well."

"What is the matter with him?"

"He fears everyone, and he just wants to escape. He doesn't want to be here. He seems especially scared of me."

"Of you?" I asked confused. "Doesn't he realize that you saved him?"

"I don't think so, no."

"Can I come over today?"

"Are you sure you want that? How are you feeling by the way? Still sick?"

"I feel a little hot … and my head hurts a bit," I replied, "but I think it's getting better."

"Oh, good! I suppose you can come over then, it's just that I need to stay with Oliver and it's not exactly a tea party in here."

"That's okay, it doesn't have to be," I chuckled.

"Your choice," she said. "Oh, yeah, Amaeka wanted to talk to you. Why don't I ask her to come fetch you?"

"Sure, how about an hour or so from now?"

"Great, see you then, bye!"

"Bye," I said and hung up. I got out of bed, wrapped my robe around myself and went downstairs for breakfast, using my new crutches that my mum had brought for me. No one was home but there was a note on the counter.

'Mum is sleeping, I'm at grandmas. I put some money in your jacket pocket in case you need it. See you tonight. Love, Dad'

I couldn't help but smile a little and I made myself a smoothie, relieved to have the option to do so. After I drank it all I took another shower, a longer one this time to really make sure I was clean after last week, practiced some much needed selfcare and got dressed. Being able to perform a normal morning routine again felt like a gift. Feeling satisfied and confident, I went outside and saw Amaeka was already waiting for me.

"Hi," we said awkwardly at the same time; since the two of us hadn't been alone yet and didn't really know each other, it felt a little strange.

"Everything okay?" she asked as she started walking away, so I joined her.

"I guess … It's been a while since I didn't have anyone out to kill me. I guess there's little risk now that Devlin … You know," I said. "So I guess I'm okay, you?"

"Makes one of us," she said and grinned. "Onyx and I have our own troubles. But I guess I'm okay too."

We reached the end of the street, and she made a gesture towards a car. There was a click and the car doors unlocked. She got in and so did I, putting my crutches beside me.

"So … someone is trying to kill you?" I asked as I put my seat belt on.

"Vampires aren't supposed to be partnered with werewolves," she said as she put hers on too, then started the car. "They think we are beneath them. To most of them our marriage is just as much of a threat as humans knowing that vampires exist. They don't care that we were already married when Onyx was bitten, against his will too."

"Oh," I said. "They have a lot of rules, don't they?"

"Yeah," she said as she drove away, "and they take them way too far."

I nodded in agreement.

"Sorry for coming off so strong," she said and laughed a little embarrassed. "I don't meet many people like you. I guess I got a little excited."

"That's okay," I said and laughed too. "What do you mean people like me? I guess Onyx told you …?"

"Yeah, he told me how you got bitten, but that's not really what I mean. I'm around other wolves all the time but I don't meet many who are … Who see vampires as equals."

I still didn't really know what she meant, so we were both silent for a moment.

"There is this expectation, this hierarchy among certain beings," Amaeka continued, "werewolves and vampires aren't enemies, but it is expected that we should always come second to them. We are supposed to bow to them if you will; never intervene. Relationships are out of the question because we are not equal, at least in their eyes. Unfortunately, all the wolves I know just obey this stupid ancient idea too."

"Wow … Why?"

"It's always the immortality thing. They're so weird about it. You should see how they treat vampire children."

I had never seen that, of course, but Bluebell had given me an idea about it. Vampires supposedly worshipped vampire children because they were seen as the epitome of immortality, they had eternal youth and they would physically never even reach adulthood.

"Anyway," she continued once more, her dark eyes on the road, "luckily Onyx doesn't buy any of it. And Bluebell, of course, she must be the most rebellious vampire I've ever met. But they are the only ones I know of who kind of disobey those rules."

"So you don't know any other werewolves who …?"

"I did once. They're dead now."

I looked at her thunderstruck for a few seconds. "Oh."

"Vampires. They disrespected them and they were killed."

She cast me a quick look.

"They let you off because you're no longer human, so your knowing about their existence is no longer a threat. But you are

166

expected to never get involved with a vampire, never disrespect them and never tell a human about their existence, or you're still dead. They are the elite."

I looked out of the window and felt my courage sink a bit. I thought that now I was no longer considered a meal, and out from under the curse, I could stop feeling scared, stop feeling like I always had to look over my shoulder; and maybe I could, but now I had to always think about other things to make sure I wouldn't step out of line.

"Bluebell will protect you," Amaeka eventually said. "It's best to just stay away from vampires, other than she and Onyx. Stay out of their way and you'll probably be able to stay out of trouble."

The car slowed down, and she parked it on a small parking lot. I could see the entrance to a forest beside us.

"We have to walk from here," she said as she started getting out of the car. I followed her lead. She locked the car and we walked into the forest slowly so I could keep up. The forest was huge, wild, and seemed to be mostly untouched by humans.

"Beautiful, isn't it?" asked Amaeka, as she looked around her.

"Yes, absolutely," I said as I also looked around, not having seen much of it in daylight. "So ..." Before I could ask anything, she smiled at me.

"You must have a lot of questions. Go ahead."

I smiled gratefully. "Were you born a werewolf or were you bitten?"

"Born," she answered proudly, "I come from a long line of werewolves. My mother was the first in generations to have a child with a human, but there's no such thing as half-werewolves or anything. If one of your parents is a wolf, so are you."

"When does it ... start?"

"Right away."

"Really?"

"Yeah. New-born babies will just be new-born pups and so on."

"Is it true that some werewolves can choose to transform?" I asked, while attempting to avoid putting my crutches down on acorns and pinecones.

She chuckled. "No, it's not. Werewolves are werewolves and shapeshifters are shapeshifters. They're not the same."

We walked in silence for a moment as I let the information sink in.

"The next full moon will be in about a month. Are you excited?" Amaeka asked eventually.

"Should I be?" I asked. I had only been told that it hurt, and the book Rosabella gave me said many things about blood thirst. It didn't exactly sound like a good time.

"Why not? You get to be a wolf for a night. It's beautiful," she said, as she looked at me with a twinkle in her eyes. "The forests, the moon, how you can suddenly run faster than you ever guessed ... You can't get any closer to nature than that."

"I heard that it hurts," I said nervously, "and that you become thirsty for blood."

She frowned for a moment. "Well, your entire skeleton changes form ... Of course, it's going to hurt a little bit. But it lasts like, what, thirty seconds? And you don't suddenly become thirsty for blood. That's a vampire thing. Of course you're bound to get hungry sometime in the night and some of us hunt. You don't have to, though. Most of us just wait it out instead. *Of course* you're not excited if this is all you've been told," she said and laughed. "I'm glad we're having this talk."

"It does sound a little better now," I said as I gave her a faint smile. "How does it happen? The transformation? Do you have to stand in the moonlight?"

She nodded. "Once the full moon light falls on you it starts. And when the first morning sunlight falls on you, you transform back."

"I see," I said, still attempting to dodge pinecones, then I frowned. "But if you transform back once the moon is gone, how come I was bitten during the day?"

Amaeka stopped in her tracks and looked at me very confused. "You were bitten during the day?"

"Yeah," I said, also having stopped walking, a little startled by her response.

"That's not right," she said, frowning, and set off walking again. "It doesn't work like that."

We kept on walking in silence for a moment until she shrugged. "Onyx and Bluebell would've noticed if you were bitten by anything other than a werewolf. It's just odd how it happened … We'll have to talk to Bluebell about this. Maybe the wolf who bit you was on some sort of potion as well."

I nodded, not sure what to do with this information.

"So, uhm, when we were all talking, we, uhm, thought that maybe you'd like to stay with us for a bit," Amaeka said shyly. "So you can … adjust."

"With you and Onyx?" I asked surprised.

"Yeah! I can guide you and you can meet my pack. You'll be one of us."

I looked at the path we were walking on. It was a nice offer but?

"Of course, Bluebell will be there too," she added as she noticed that I was looking away. "We already talked about that, don't worry. Besides, we both figured it would be better for Oliver to be in a domestic setting instead of her bunker. It's not very … welcoming."

"Oh," I answered. "I'll think about it, then. Some help would be nice, I suppose."

"Great," said Amaeka happily. "I could have everything ready for you by tonight, just let me know."

As we continued walking, we strayed off the path and started walking through the dense trees, going down a hill (me struggling immensely) and walking where I was sure no one would be hiking. Eventually I saw a familiar tree that looked kind of funny and from the ground, as if it weren't there before, a latch overgrown by plants opened. Bluebell's head was poking out.

"Look! Amaeka got us stairs!"

I chuckled. We walked over to the bunker, and I noticed that Bluebell was standing on a ladder. She went down so Amaeka and I could climb down, and I immediately noticed there was also a decent lamp so I could see properly for the first time.

In one of the corners, Oliver was sitting as far away as possible from Rosabella and Onyx. He was clearly on edge, sitting still but keeping an eye on everyone. His eyes shifted to me and Amaeka the second we came in. Not sure how to greet him, I gave him a faint smile and a nod and then turned towards the others, who greeted me with hugs, except for Rosabella who gave me a similar smile and nod as I had just given Oliver.

"Oli, this is Junie," Bluebell started, trying to properly introduce us. "She was also there last night, remember? She is a good friend of mine."

He didn't give any type of response, just stared at us with a blank expression on his face.

"She already knows who you are," she continued. "I hope you two will get along." Bluebell then turned to me.

"He hasn't spoken," she said, sounding a bit defeated. "He keeps as much distance as he can."

"You said he tried to escape, how is that going?"

"He's calmed down since the sun came up," she sighed. "I'm afraid that tonight he'll start trying again. We'll also need to feed him tonight though, and we want to get him to the house ..."

"How are you going to do that?" I was almost whispering to Bluebell, but she didn't seem to even try to keep her voice down and talked about Oliver as if he wasn't there.

"We can't let him out of our sight ... We'll have to bring him food, we'll work that out. Honestly, I'm more worried about getting him to the house. Have you decided yet if you'll come?"

"I think I will," I said, feeling more at peace with the idea now that I was with Bluebell again. It actually felt kind of exciting. "But I can't come tonight. I'll have to talk to my parents and pack and everything."

"Great! Then I'll get your room ready too," said Amaeka, happily inserting herself in our conversation. "I'll see you all later and see you when you're ready."

She winked at me, went to give her husband a kiss and then climbed up the ladder again and disappeared. Oliver's blank eyes followed her until the latch was shut again, then his eyes landed on Bluebell and stayed there.

Chapter Twenty-Two

One Hundred and Seventy One

That night, at dinner with my parents, I broke the news that I wasn't coming with them when they moved.

"I just think I'm ready to be on my own again," I said as I poked my fork into my seitan sausage patty.

"That's great, dear, but please stay out of trouble," my father answered, clearly still worried about Bluebell being the cause of all the trouble.

"Where was this house again?" asked my mother.

"It's near Noctiluca woods."

"At least you'll be out of this town," said my mother. I nodded.

"Well, I know you've already made up your mind, but I would be greatly relieved if I could meet these … other friends of yours," said my father as he gave me a faint smile.

"Maybe we could see the house?" my mother asked.

"Of course," I said as I smiled. "I'll call them right after dinner and maybe we can all go over there and have tea tomorrow."

And so, we went over for afternoon tea the next day. Bluebell had stayed in her bunker with Oliver, accompanied by Rosabella – they had waited to move him since they didn't want him near any humans. To the people of Cunabula he was nothing short of a murderer on the loose so they couldn't risk anyone seeing him, especially since no one knew whether he could control himself well enough around people. Bluebell didn't want to leave her brother's side – so, much to my father's frustration, she wasn't at the house that day. Rosabella didn't have to be introduced, they didn't need to know about her, nor did we tell them she would also technically be living there since she was always around Bluebell.

Rosabella could turn into a tiny spiderling if she needed to and not attract any attention.

At around four p.m. my parents and I were having tea with Onyx and Amaeka in their house, and they were totally unaware of being in the house with mythical beings and ignorant of the fact that I hadn't seen the house before either. Of course, I said I had, but I was just as impressed by it as my parents were.

The house was rather large and stood on an even larger piece of land. The nearest neighbours were several minutes driving distance away. The land had no fences around it, but looked like an extension of the nearby forest. There were many trees on the grassland and no sign of any type of paving humans normally liked to have in their gardens. It was as natural as it could be.

The inside was tidy, clean and despite the size still rather cosy but it was decorated in a way that was also clearly appreciative of nature. There was lots of wood (recycled wood, of course, Amaeka told me in almost an offended tone even though I hadn't said anything at all). There were tons of plants, and the room was designed so that as much natural light as possible came through the huge, tall windows. It made sense to me that this was the house of someone who was born a werewolf. To my amusement, the wall across from me had a full moon for a clock.

"Thank you again for having us over," said my mother.

"Our pleasure," answered Amaeka warmly.

Onyx nodded along with her. He was as always dressed in black, looking rather vampy just from his style and his hair was as polished as ever. He did appear to have fixed his teeth as they looked like regular human teeth without two- to three-inch-long fangs. He was wearing bright blue contacts, the exact colour that Bluebell always wore, so his eyes looked human too.

The only noticeably odd thing about him at this moment was his restlessness. He was letting Amaeka do most of the talking and he excused himself more than one normally would.

"Such a lovely place," my father said as he looked around.

"Thank you," said Amaeka as she smiled. "We love it here and the location is great too." Onyx was nodding along again.

"Absolutely!" agreed my mother. "Well, there is no doubt in my mind that you have enough spare room for our Junie."

"With everything going on, we just want to make sure that she's okay," my father chimed in. "You two seem like decent folks."

Amaeka smiled warmly and Onyx did his best to do the same.

"So how do you all know each other?" asked my mother while looking at Onyx, trying to engage him in conversation. Onyx was startled by this.

"We met through Bluebell," said Onyx as if he had rehearsed this.

"Oh," said my mother. "It's a shame we haven't been introduced sooner."

"I'm glad Junie found a friend in her ... I do worry that she always seems to get herself in some kind of trouble," admitted my father.

"Don't worry about that, Mr Lunis," said Amaeka consolingly. "Bluebell is always eager to help and sometimes acts a little impulsively but it's all good-natured. Besides, we'll keep an eye on her."

Amaeka winked at me, and I smiled gratefully at her. My father seemed to be a little bit consoled by this.

"Speaking of that ... I heard you chased that man out of the garlic shop yesterday, but you lost him," my mother said to Onyx. "Of course we went out to look for him but couldn't find him. Would you two mind coming over to the station tomorrow to discuss the situation? We have a lot of questions that you may be able to help us out with. We'd like you and Bluebell to come over as well, Junie; and that other woman who was with you as well, she was a friend of yours too I believe?"

"We'd be happy to help," said Amaeka, "and yes, she is our friend. We'll ask her to come along."

I was lost for words for a moment, anxiety-struck, not understanding how we were going to pull this off, but while Amaeka continued to converse with my parents, Onyx, who was still silent as much as he could be, locked eyes with me. The look he gave me was one of understanding and reassurance.

We spent the next hour or so talking about the house, me moving in, what Amaeka, Onyx and Bluebell did for a living (apparently Amaeka ran a dog rescue non-profit and Onyx worked night shifts as some sort of security guard, we told my parents that Bluebell was a student who was studying something about nature, just like she had once told me) and what work I was going to do to support myself; Amaeka suggested a job at a local animal shelter that she worked with that was hiring. We also talked about how my parents were also looking to move, the situation in Cunabula that all of us were speaking very vaguely about and eventually, we received a tour of the house. Every room had the same earthly feel to it. The only rooms that were off-limits were the basement and one bedroom upstairs, that Amaeka claimed were just too messy for visitors to see. She showed my parents and me the room I would be sleeping in. It was a spacious bedroom, just like the rest of the house. It had big windows and next to one of them was a single bed, all done up with patterned sheets and several comfortable looking pillows.

On the way home, my parents seemed to be at peace with me moving in with my friends and they were talking about what a nice couple Amaeka and Onyx were. Of course, we had to lie to them about how long we had known each other.

They also spoke of how they loved their house and how it gave them ideas for what they wanted in their new house. This continued all throughout our dinner. Once I made my way upstairs and threw myself on my bed, I got a call from Bluebell asking how it went.

"I think they were very impressed by everything."

"It is an impressive house. I'm happy to hear that it went so well! How did Onyx do?"

"He was miserable," I said and chuckled. "Was it because ... ?"

"Yeah, he avoids being around people. It's hard when people make you feel like you've been starved for weeks ... Anyway, I wanted to talk to you about tomorrow. Rosa is not coming. She must stay with Oliver and besides, she's not registered anywhere. So, it'll be the four of us.

The story is that I went in to help, because apparently, I have this irresistible urge to try to save the day," – I chuckled as she spoke –, "and Oliver is unknown to us all. We don't know who he is, we don't know his name, he ran away, and Onyx and Rosa tried to chase him. Amaeka joined them later, but they lost him and went home exhausted. Rosabella eventually disappeared, maybe she is the next murder victim or something and we'll figure that out."

"What about the fact that their bullets didn't hurt him? And what about Devlin? What do we say happened inside?"

"We arrived when Devlin was already dead. We don't know what happened to his body and we sure don't know anything about how a dragon appeared. Didn't even know they were real."

That part would be true for me, I thought.

"We don't know why bullets didn't work. We don't know why he was so out of control. I just tried to help, and you all wanted to protect me and my hero complex. He tried to attack us too and then ran out. As far as we know he is indeed a lunatic who needs to be caught but we don't know any more than they do."

We kept that story up the next day, letting Bluebell do most of the talking and me agreeing and chiming in when I felt I wouldn't screw up. Onyx was miserable again and looking at every single human in fear, trying to compose himself but staring obsessively.

"Don't mind my husband," explained Amaeka, "he was the one who got attacked by that man last night. He is very shaken."

It wasn't my mother doing the interview as they wanted someone unbiased to talk to us.

"Hm … So, Ms Solstice, you claim you ran in simply because you wanted to help?" asked the interviewer with one of her blonde eyebrows raised.

"Yes, ma'am," Bluebell answered, trying to sound ashamed.

"And you didn't know this man who you were trying to help?"

"I was trying to help the police, not him. Ms Marcelin …"

"I know you know Ms Marcelin, but you really thought you would be better equipped to help her rather than an entire armed police force? Why would you think that? Were you armed as well?"

"No … I just heard that the bullets didn't seem to affect him, and I felt like I needed to do something. I realize this was stupidly impulsive."

"Right," said the officer, "and Ms Lunis-Marcelin, you ran after your friend because you wanted to help her?"

"Yes, ma'am, I agree that my friend was acting dangerously and impulsively. For that very reason I felt that I had to look out for her. My other friends felt the same way," I said as I made a hand gesture towards Amaeka and Onyx.

"Aha … And where is your fourth friend, Ms Lunis-Marcelin? I believe there was someone else with you?"

"When we went to chase after that dangerous man, we lost her. We lost track of him, he was just too fast. So then we called out and went to look for our friend, but she wasn't there. We think maybe he took her," said Amaeka in a worried voice.

The policewoman raised both of her eyebrows this time.

"That is very curious indeed. What is this woman's name?"

"Bella … Bright," said Bluebell as I noticed her scanning the room and squinting at the bright lights on the ceiling.

"We'll keep an eye out for your friend," she said as she wrote Rosabella's fake name down. "What happened when you chased the perpetrator? How did he get out? Describe the scenario, please."

"Like I said Ms, he attacked my husband, and luckily no damage was done," said Amaeka in a caring voice. "As we succeeded in getting him away from my husband he fled. He went through the broken window in the back and just started running. We decided to chase him, but he outran us, and we lost him."

"At what point did you realize your friend was gone?"

"When we gave up running we thought she was with us, but it was just us two."

"And you two," the interviewer said as she pointed her pen at me and then at Bluebell. "Why didn't you chase him if you were so eager to help?"

"Our friends were faster than we were and at that point we were exhausted from trying to get him to calm down. Junie broke her leg too," said Bluebell. "We wouldn't have been able to keep up."

"Aha …" the woman said as she was taking notes. "At a certain point you were seen dragging the perpetrator behind the counter where we completely lost sight of you. Why?"

"To dodge the bullets," said Onyx suddenly.

"Yes, how were you able to jump in front of the shots our force fired and be … fine?" she asked, sounding sceptical. "I personally didn't see it, but it was described to me as being quite like our … suspects abilities."

"I was wearing a bulletproof vest, ma'am."

I suppressed the urge to face palm myself. Was that the best he could come up with? The policewoman seemed unimpressed too.

"Sir, with all due respect, why would you be wearing a bulletproof vest? Why did you all come to the scene of the crime to begin with? Where were you when it started?"

"Please excuse my husband's sarcastic comment, Ms, he has a strange sense of humour," said Amaeka. "My husband was never actually hit. He managed to dodge all of the bullets."

"My sources would disagree," said the policewoman sternly as she took more notes.

I could see Onyx eyeing the clock on the wall. The interviewer noticed this when she looked back up and opened her mouth to say something about it, but then Bluebell started talking.

"Anything else, ma'am?"

She turned to Bluebell. "Yes – Ms Solstice and Ms Lunis-Marcelin, you two have recently given a statement that described someone who we believe could be the same person as the person involved in an unfortunate casualty that happened last night."

All of us pretended to be shocked.

"I'm sure some of you saw a black sheet covering someone's body outside where the window was broken," she continued unimpressed. "The deceased, who was murdered by the man inside the shop, matches the description you gave us a while ago. This man was blond, a hundred and ninety centimetres tall, who did not take care of himself well and had white eyes with no pupils." She waited for a response and when no one responded, she continued; I figured there was no way to let us identify him whatsoever, so she couldn't tell us much more.

"The man inside the store had white eyes too. Did you recognize this man?" she continued.

"No," said Bluebell while I shook my head. Onyx and Amaeka shook their heads too.

"Okay," she said as she looked down at her notes again and wrote something.

"Why did you ..." she pointed at Amaeka with her pen, "... and your friend try to stop the police from firing shots at the suspect and going inside?" she was speaking as if the question was routine and boring.

"We thought we were making progress with overpowering him, he seemed to be getting tired. We didn't want our progress to get lost," answered Amaeka confidently.

"Right, right ..." she continued, sounding bored. "Now, where did this man run off to when you couldn't keep up anymore?"

"We think he ran off into the forest."

I felt that this was a risky move, as Rosabella was hiding Oliver down in the bunker inside the forest closest to the store at that very moment. I figured there wasn't much choice as the other option would be him running down into the town and then it would be easy to find out whether we were lying.

The policewoman scribbled down some more notes.

"That will be all. You're free to go. If you see any sign of this man, please contact us immediately. Thank you."

She got up while casting one last suspicious glare at Onyx, who was pinching the arms of the chair he was in and she walked out, leaving the door open for us. Onyx instantly seemed more relaxed as she walked out.

"Let's go home," Amaeka said as she looked at Onyx sympathetically. He gave her a grateful smile.

We all got up and walked out, making our way to Amaeka's car.

"So, they are really not going to mention anything about a dragon and a body disappearing?" asked Amaeka as she put her seatbelt on, the rest of us following.

"Nope," said Bluebell. "Bet she'll be under fire from the other shapeshifters, though, for doing all that. No pun intended."

We all chuckled.

"Should I drive you home, Junie? Reckon you want to start packing?"

"That'd be great, thank you."

Amaeka drove us to the edge of Saecula forest; firstly, to drop off Bluebell so she could go back to her brother.

"What's the plan?" asked Onyx as the car slowed down. He was a completely different person than he was when I first met him, it seemed as if he wasn't as used to being around humans as Bluebell was and had to fight hard to control himself. He was still pulling himself back together and was not his usual bubbly self.

"We have to move him tonight," said Bluebell matter-of-factly. "We can't risk it if they're going to search the forest. Can you be there at midnight, Onyx?"

He nodded.

"We'll move him and then I'll have to hunt afterwards," said Onyx.

Bluebell nodded in understanding. "Yeah, I have to hunt too … We'll move him; then you go, and I'll go after you're back. Stay out of the area."

"Sure thing. I'll take care of the kid too. See you tonight, Blue."

"Great, thank you. Text me," she said to me as she undid her seat belt and scooted over to the door.

"Will do, keep me updated!"

Bluebell got out, walked the path into the forest, looked around to see if anyone was there and when she didn't see anyone she started running at superhuman speed and disappeared.

Amaeka started the car again and they drove me home.

"Let me know if you need help packing tomorrow, love," Amaeka said, as she looked at me in the rear-view mirror.

The next day was Saturday and we decided I would move that same night. My father was at home, and he helped me to pack my stuff. I invited Amaeka too, even though I didn't really need her help. Most of my stuff was still in boxes from when I moved back in with my parents. I mostly invited Amaeka so I had someone to fall back on when it came to talking about everything, she was good with words. To my surprise, however; my father didn't mention anything and seemed to be avoiding talking about anything other than gathering my stuff. This continued after my exhausted mother came home from work with her glasses crooked on her nose and she too avoided talking about anything unusual. When my parents went to cook dinner, I closed my bedroom door to talk to Amaeka.

"What was that all about?" I wondered aloud. "They are never that non-committal."

Amaeka shrugged. "Well, at least we won't have to follow a script then."

I grinned. "How did everything go last night? I texted Bluebell, but she hasn't responded yet. Did everything go okay?"

"It uhm, it worked out in the end. Everyone is at the house. Your parents won't see him, don't worry," she reassured me as she saw my slightly worried expression. "But it was a struggle. He kept trying to escape but ... Well, Bluebell will fill you in on the details later. It took hours to move him, Onyx barely had time to hunt, especially since he also had to go back to Larua, and Bluebell didn't get to hunt at all. I hope she gets to go tonight but Oliver might be restless because of your parents coming, so I doubt it."

"It hasn't been easy, has it? I reckon this is not what she expected when she found Oliver. It's not a happy reunion."

"You're right about that," answered Amaeka.

Dinner was a spicy soup and unlike the food, the atmosphere was very dull. My parents were so keen on avoiding conversation that they barely talked at all.

Then my mother's phone rang. She got up to answer the call and disappeared for a few minutes. She came back to the table and let out a sigh.

"I'm sorry, dear, I have to go," she said regretfully.

"What happened?" I asked curiously.

She looked hesitantly at my father for a few seconds. "Well … It seems like the suspect has moved on to another town. There are more victims and their identities have just been confirmed. I have to go over there."

"Victims? Plural?" asked Amaeka.

"Yes, it's quite odd, really … It happened all the way over in Malitia. That is hours away from here … Why would a killer relocate that far away, just to continue? Anyway, I'm sorry I can't see you off, dear," said my mother. "I'll come and visit soon, okay?"

I nodded. "Of course, Mum, no problem."

She stared out the window regretfully for a moment.

"Are you okay, Ms?" asked Amaeka.

"Yes," she said and sighed. "I just don't understand … The victims are three children. Two of them are barely a year old."

My father looked at her sympathetically. "You're doing everything you can to catch them, honey."

"Thank you," she said and gave him a faint smile. "Well, I should be going then. I'll see you soon, sweetheart. Please take care of her."

That last part was directed at Amaeka, who gave her a reassuring nod.

My mother got her coat and walked out the door.

A while later I was in the car with my father while Amaeka drove in front of us in hers, to lead the way. I left the things that were unnecessary at my parents' house – since I was moving into yet another house that wasn't my own, I didn't need to bring that much. Everything I needed fitted into my father's car. We arrived at Amaeka and Onyx's place and started unloading my bags and a few boxes and brought them to my new bedroom. Onyx and Bluebell helped us unload and I figured that Rosabella was keeping Oliver company, wherever in the house he might be.

After some tea and a goodbye from my father, I sat down on one of the couches in the living room and Amaeka went to close the automated blinds.

Bluebell and the once again restless Onyx went off to check on Oliver.

"Where is he, anyway?" I asked Amaeka.

"He is in the basement. It's dark and quiet there. We were preparing it for him so we couldn't let your folks see it."

"What is there to see?" I asked curiously.

"A massive freezer stuffed with dead animals just in case," she said, while she sat down across from me, "and a couch. We've soundproofed it all. But most importantly, there is a silver door so he won't just run off."

I couldn't help but feel bad them. Both for Oliver and the animals in the freezer.

Moments later, Rosabella, Onyx, Bluebell and Oliver all walked into the living room. Onyx and Bluebell were arm in arm with Oliver, who looked as uncomfortable and out of place as anyone could be. They sat down on the couch next to Amaeka, both of them still holding Oliver. Rosabella sat down next to me on the other couch.

"Oli, Junie is here now, she's going to stay with us, remember?" Bluebell said with a smile.

I couldn't help but pity her – the love she had for her brother seemed out of this world, but he seemed completely unresponsive. He fixed his eyes on me.

Onyx brought his free hand to his eyes and took out the bright blue contacts.

"I hate these things," he mumbled as he looked at them on his fingers, seeming unsure of what to do with them.

Amaeka quickly got up and fetched a container with contact lens fluid from somewhere and Onyx put them in it. Bluebell followed his lead.

"How come you don't wear them again?" asked Bluebell. "You can't possibly go to work bare-eyed?"

"Bare-eyed?" I asked amused. Bluebell chuckled, so did Onyx.

"Yeah ... Well, I just wear thick sunglasses, I barely run into people. If I do, they don't question it."

"Huh," said Bluebell, slightly fascinated.

"So how did it go last night?" I asked curiously, not knowing who exactly to ask, so I just shifted my eyes between everyone. Bluebell looked at Oliver.

"Not so smooth. We, uhm, found something out. Something happened. Could you show her your scar, Oli?"

Without breaking his intense stare at me and without saying a word, he lifted his arm and rolled up his sleeve. I was surprised to see him respond, albeit without talking.

There, on his bicep, was a massive scar, unmistakably due to a bite. It looked as if a whole chunk of his arm had been taken out.

"You can put it down again," said Bluebell as Oliver was keeping his arm out without showing any intention of putting it back. He rolled his sleeve back down and relaxed his arm.

"What happened?"

"Well ... Amaeka and Rosa emptied the bunker first, then Onyx and I took him out. He was thrilled to go out. He seemed to be calm but then he suddenly started to run," Bluebell said as she was looking at Oliver again, who was still just staring me down. "Well, he tried to run. He couldn't. He just fell and started screaming and shaking. After a moment, he got up, composed himself and then he tried again. It happened again. We didn't know what was wrong, but he started scratching his arm open and tore his shirt. So we checked his arm and ..."

"And the number one hundred and seventy-one was on his bicep," continued Onyx. "Something was in there that he wasn't rejecting, so Bluebell took it out."

"What was it?!"

"I ... I don't know. It looked like some sort of capsule. It was zapping him and shocking him but it was also pushing out the number, you know like what a stamp looks like from underneath? But it was pure silver."

"We think it worked like a shock collar, kind of," said Bluebell, "like he was being tracked somehow and corrected, like a pawn. The police didn't specify exactly what happened, but it could be that that was why he never made it out of the store."

"Like someone is watching what he's doing and keeping him in place? Do you think it's Ubel?" I asked.

"I don't know ... He is vile but I don't know if he is *this* organized and deliberate. He's just an asshole. Anyway, we removed and destroyed the thing, so I reckon that part is over. Whoever was playing games with him shouldn't be able to anymore."

"Terrible as it was, at least he doesn't seem to be so eager to escape anymore," said Onyx while scanning Oliver, their arms still intertwined but Oliver showing no reason to be needing to be held like that.

Bluebell nodded. "Let's hope he won't."

"Well," said Onyx, letting Oliver go and getting up. "I am starving so I will go now. Enjoy your first night here, Junie. I'll see you all tomorrow."

"Stay away from Malitia," said Amaeka. "They found three eaten bodies over there. You don't want to draw any more attention."

"Three bodies in one place? They're getting so careless these days," said Onyx irritably.

"Yeah, well ... Either they're weak or they're playing some kind of game," continued Amaeka. "Esther said two out of the three victims were one-year olds and the other one was a child too."

Bluebell looked at her as if she had just insulted her ancestors.

"Junie, could you please call your mother?" she asked tensely. Everyone looked at her curiously.

"Check if the other kid is seven years old. If they're playing a game it may involve us."

"Oh, one hundred and seventy one!" exclaimed Onyx. "Good catch."

So, I called my mother, doing my best to sound interested in the case without any secret motive, while also sounding like I was just calling to tell her I was all settled in the new house. I managed to find out that the other child was, indeed, seven years old.

"They want me to go there," said Bluebell matter-of-factly, once I hung up.

We all nodded silently. It had to be the truth.

"I don't think I will, though," she added. "Oli is here; unless they put some more of their crap in him and they're somehow the only ones who can get it out, I see no reason to go."

"Do you think it'll just be over like that …?" asked Rosabella.

"Let's find out," answered Bluebell. "I'm just going to lie low and focus on him getting better. Junie should be safe, Oli should be safe. I'm not going to risk anything if I don't have to."

"Very understandable," said Amaeka.

"I'm off then," repeated Onyx as he walked up to Amaeka to kiss her and then went out the door.

"I'm going to defrost something for myself from that freezer downstairs," said Bluebell with a sigh. "I don't reckon Oliver is going to try anything but I'll be back up in a second if he does."

So Bluebell disappeared to the basement.

"Yeah, and I'm going to call it a night," said Rosabella, sounding tired. "See you all tomorrow."

Rosabella walked away as well.

"Can I get you anything, Junie? Do you want some more tea?" asked Amaeka.

"That would be lovely, thank you," I answered.

So Amaeka got up as well and walked to the kitchen, leaving Oliver and myself alone in the living room. I decided to take this opportunity to try and console him a little bit, disturbed as he looked, and of course, still staring me down.

"Look, Oliver, I completely understand that you're scared," I said, speaking softly while looking back at him. "I just want you to know that we're not out to hurt you."

He didn't respond in any way, as I expected, so I continued.

"I hope you'll believe it soon. I, uhm … I just want you to be okay, that's all."

"I know," Oliver answered.

Chapter Twenty-Three

Full Circle

I stared at Oliver thunderstruck. He hadn't spoken once since we found him, not a single word, not even when he was being cut open by sharp fangs, or bleeding out, or having his organs exposed.

"... What?" was all I managed to get out.

He chuckled. "I know you don't have any ill will," he said casually, as if he hadn't been completely silent for days.

"Why are you talking to me?" I asked in a whisper.

At that moment, Amaeka came back into the living room with a pot of tea and Oliver went back to not speaking. A moment later Bluebell came back from downstairs, looking more relaxed. We all sat together for a while, Amaeka and I enjoyed a cup of tea and not too long afterwards I went up to my new bedroom and got into bed.

Thinking everything over, this was the first time I realized how well I had been sleeping, with or without Bluebell. I was okay when she wasn't around. I could sleep. I didn't want to hurt myself anymore. I didn't feel the overwhelming desperation anymore. I was indeed free.

With that thought, I fell into a deep, undisturbed sleep, even the images of Devlin's dead body and Oliver's lifeless guts did not disturb my night.

I was feeling happy again. I didn't feel the need to smoke anymore, I was sleeping well, I was no longer being dragged around or locked in a bunker to escape anyone, no one died ... Everything seemed to be going well.

Oliver wasn't trying to escape anymore and Onyx and Bluebell even took him out hunting, which had also gone well. He hadn't spoken again, since the last time, nor did I tell anyone that he had spoken to me, out of fear that he wouldn't do it again if he found out. The number one hundred and seventy one hadn't been mentioned again by anyone.

My parents had come to visit once or twice and this time Onyx had made sure to be out of the house, no matter the time of day. My father had warmed up to Bluebell once again and they seemed content with me living in my new place. Neither of my parents talked to me about the case of Cunabula and seemed to be avoiding the subject at all cost and, honestly, I was relieved.

I had been spending my time in the house talking to everyone about the mythical world I had been brought into, resting my leg and trying to prepare for the full moon. Amaeka told me not to worry about finding a job – that would come once I was adjusted.

She gave me a gentle reminder that Onyx, Bluebell and Oliver didn't eat – or have any normal bodily functions at all – so there wasn't much money spent to support everyone, and they could easily take care of me for as long as needed. Bluebell accidentally revealed to me that she was able to pay for the things she did use, like her contacts and tools, and occasionally new clothes, because of the money she found on the people who ended up being her dinner.

When it was about a week before the full moon, I started to get sick, just like everyone had predicted. It wasn't a type of sick I was used to, however. I did feel feverish and I was sweating a lot, although I differed between feeling overwhelmingly hot and freezing cold but mostly, I felt sore. I could feel something inside my body happening that I had never felt before. It was like my bones were … adjusting. I could feel the deepest parts of my body preparing themselves for something that they knew would happen, and knew exactly how it would happen and what they needed to do. As if it were simply biology.

"There you go," said Bluebell as she put a tray in my lap with a bowl of hot soup on it.

She sat down next to me. It was the morning of the full moon and we were all sitting in the living room, including Amaeka, who was working from home since she also started having symptoms, only hers seemed less severe and she was unmistakably used to it and prepared for it. She wasn't eating soup but was drinking a jug of hot, fresh tea, while working on her laptop, occasionally mumbling something about people being too thick to understand anyone other than their own species.

On the TV was a movie about mythical creatures, werewolves in specific, to make me feel more in touch with and ready for what was about to happen.

Rosabella was munching on some popcorn while watching. Onyx was watching it too with a frown on his face as if he didn't understand anything that was going on in the movie or like he simply wasn't amused by it. Bluebell and Oliver were watching it silently with Oliver still having the same, dead look on his face and I was attempting to sip some of my soup.

We spent the rest of the day like that, only broken up by Amaeka finishing her work or at least putting her laptop aside and Onyx and Rosabella getting up to make dinner for Amaeka, Rosabella and myself. They made a noodle soup with exaggerated amounts of edamame beans and tofu 'for preparation'. After dinner (and chia pudding) Amaeka came to sit next to me.

"It's almost time," she said while gazing at the setting sun through the tall windows. "We ought to go into the forest."

I nodded nervously, at this point it felt like my bones were made of hot metal, stinging from the inside. We changed into old clothes, on Amaeka's insistence. She grabbed a backpack and we went outside into the front yard. Bluebell came with us to see us off and the two of us set off for the forest. We got into Amaeka's car and drove away.

I felt awfully … naked, literally not having brought anything with me.

"There are four packs who rule this forest," said Amaeka as she looked at the road happily. "We have the north side. Coincidentally that is the side of this entrance so we will be meeting the others soon."

Within minutes we parked at the edge of the forest and started going in, Amaeka looking pitiful at me struggling to walk on my crutches over the forest ground.

"Are they okay with me being here?" I asked.

"Of course," she said consolingly while resting her eyes on me. "I will introduce you. A friend of mine is a friend of theirs."

"Okay," I said nervously. "And the other packs? Do we avoid them?"

"We just stay on our side unless there is a good reason not to. We live in harmony here."

Like Amaeka had said, after only a few minutes of walking we came across someone who Amaeka seemed to recognize.

"Dante!" she exclaimed happily.

"Amaeka," he answered as he walked up to us. Dante was a middle-aged man, or werewolf, with wavy, shoulder length black hair and warm reddish-brown skin. He simply gave me a nod and we continued to walk in silence. As we walked we picked up two more people who joined silently. One of them was a white, pale, brunette girl with big, green eyes who I estimated to be no older than fifteen years. She wore her long hair in two braids. She was petite and her name was, fittingly, Pixie. The other was a little boy, who couldn't have been much older than ten. His name was Callan. He looked a lot like Pixie and I assumed they were brother and sister.

I felt a little uneasy seeing two children out on their own at night, in the deep of a forest but Amaeka and Dante didn't seem to think anything of it.

The way we were walking led us to a clearing in the forest where several other people were gathered. Children, adults, elderly folks...

We hadn't spoken a word to each other during the walk except for the brief greetings. Now that we had arrived at the clearing, no one at all seemed to speak a word to anyone.

I noticed we were gathered in a circle.

After a moment, someone came walking out of the trees and made her way to the middle of the circle.

"Goodnight, everyone," the woman said happily, still no one replied.

Several people were smiling, however. Then Dante walked away from us and stood behind the woman, still without saying a word.

"I see a new face," she said as her brown eyes fell on me and my stomach turned. Everyone else turned to look at me as well, definitely not making me feel any more comfortable.

"This here is Junie," said Amaeka calmly. "I ask that she may join our pack. She was bitten mere weeks ago and this is her first full moon. She's in need of a pack."

"Very well," said the woman and she smiled. "Welcome to the pack, then, Junie."

That's it? I thought to myself. *It was that easy?*

"I trust that Amaeka is a good judge of character," the woman continued, noticing my discomfort. "My name is Mayu. I am the alpha of this pack. I believe you've met Dante, he is the beta of this pack. We welcome you."

"Thank you," I said softly, to which both Mayu and Dante smiled and gave me a nod.

"Let us all have a good night and look out for each other," Mayu said, and apparently that was the end of it because after she finished speaking, everyone turned to each other and started talking at once, Mayu and Dante remained standing in the same place.

"It's your first time?" asked the young boy Callan, equally surprised and excited.

"Yeah, it is …"

"You'll be fine," said Pixie confidently.

And before I could reply to her, from the corner of my eye, I saw someone start to make sudden, violent movements. I was the only one to look and I saw that this person was starting to grow in size. He was starting to be covered in hair or fur, rather, and dropped over to stand on all fours.

Next to him another person started making the same violent movements and then another and another. I looked up and saw that the full moon had just started appearing from behind the trees. The people who the moonlight had shone on first where affected first and soon others followed.

I looked back to the person who had been flailing and slapping around first and now saw, not a person but a big, grey wolf, covered in beautiful, shiny fur, standing on top of ripped clothes.

Behind him were now other wolves, all different in colour.

Then, before I knew it, my body started to hurt like it had never hurt before. It felt as if I was being cut, no, as if giant knives were stabbing me from the inside out, simultaneously it felt as if my bones were somehow breaking without them snapping ... And as if the entirety of my skin was being ripped open all at once ... I involuntarily screamed, fell over and found myself lying on the floor. I caught Amaeka's eye, who just calmly looked at me for a second, apparently not being alarmed, before she flinched and she too, started making the same violent movements as everybody else was.

The pain was becoming so sharp it felt as if I was going to pass out. I only noticed I had been screaming still when I fell silent, and I started whimpering and gasping for air. I was grateful that I was lying on the ground at this point so I wouldn't fall and be in even more pain when I inevitably fainted. I was starting to see white.

My hands, my feet and oddly enough, my gums started to hurt, as if a thousand needles where piercing them, I couldn't stop myself from shaking ... And then suddenly it just stopped.

I lay still for a while, trying to catch my breath, when a wolfs head appeared over me, which I could see clearer than I had ever seen anything before at this time of the night. The dark was no longer hindering my sight. I was surprised by my own lack of instinct to get away as quickly as possible – instead I felt a feeling of ... friendship, of belonging. The wolf looked friendly somehow. I stared at it for a moment before I recognized the friendly eyes. It had to be Amaeka.

"That's right."

I blinked in confusion for a moment. I had heard her talking, but her face didn't move and ... well, she was a wolf.

"I can hear you, Junie. And you can hear me. This is how we communicate."

It was? Werewolves used telepathy?

"We do."

I realized I was still spread out on the ground, and I instinctively started trying to get up. It was unexpectedly hard, because besides having a broken leg, I now had four paws instead of two hands and two feet and all of my limbs practically worked the same instead of them having completely different functions.

I also noticed I was covered in thick, black fur. My whole body felt different and it took a moment before I found out on how to properly stand on my new legs.

Finally, I was standing steadily as best as I could and looked around. Everything was different, the colours were muted, faded and ... different. I saw that there were only a few humans left standing. I looked over at Amaeka, who was looking like a large wolf who also had black fur. Behind her I saw two smaller wolves, covered in a lighter fur. I recognized their big eyes and realized they had to be Pixie and Callan.

I looked around the forest and I saw that the two wolves in the middle were Mayu and Dante. There were now two black wolves, standing proudly, gazing over their pack. I looked around and saw wolves in all sizes and all different, but slightly muted, colours.

"Look, almost everyone is done!" said Amaeka's voice.

I looked over and saw the last pair of people making those same strange, flailing movements and eventually turn into two big, powerful looking wolves. Then I noticed them moving their heads up and I was hit by the sound of every single wolf in the pack howling in harmony. Before I could make a conscious decision, I was joining them.

"Have a good night, everyone, and remember to stay on our grounds!" I heard Mayu's voice roar at last.

The pack spread out and disappeared into the trees. Callan and Pixie were playfully wrestling and snapping at each other.

"Come on," said Amaeka's voice and I saw her jerk her head towards the trees before she started running.

I took a deep breath and prepared myself to see if I could run on these weird legs, then set off and followed her, being pleasantly surprised by my own ability and the speed I could reach with one leg mostly dangling in the air.

I followed Amaeka through the trees. I was running easier and faster than I ever had. We sped through the forest, jumped over logs and creaks tiring ourselves out before we took a break at a specific creak to drink some water.

Amaeka lay down on her stomach and looked at me. "Pretty cool, isn't it?"

It really is, I thought. Transforming had hurt beyond belief but it had been absolutely worth it. I had felt so free running through the forest that I would gladly do it again next month, never mind the fever and soreness.

Another wolf jumped over the creak we were lying next to and suddenly jumped onto a tree, attempting to climb up. Moments later I heard a small squeak and saw the wolf running away with a bleeding squirrel flapping about in its mouth.

We spent the rest of the night running, even swimming, climbing, and chasing each other and doing anything I could think of that I wanted to do that night.

Eventually, miraculously still full of energy, Amaeka led the way back to the opening where everyone else was gathered. We all sat, waiting patiently, until the morning sun rose and shone down on us; this time hitting me and Amaeka first.

I felt the excruciating pain once more, once more I fell flat on the floor, whimpering, shaking, and then it was gone again, just as quickly as it had started.

Amaeka quickly threw something over me. I absently looked at it and noticed it was a blanket. Horrified, I wrapped it around me, realizing I must've torn out of all the clothes that I was wearing. When I looked up I saw everyone getting dressed, most of them already putting their shoes on or zipping up their jackets, including Amaeka.

"Here."

She opened up the backpack she was wearing and pulled out a dress and some shoes. My dress and my shoes.

"It'll get better, I promise. You'll get used to it."

"I hope so," I said, my body aching all over.

Amaeka helped me go up behind some trees and put on my clothes, then she took the blanket back and we went back to the circle.

We were once again standing in a group of regular looking people, Mayu and Dante again standing in the middle of the circle we gathered in.

I was suddenly hit by a hunger that was unfamiliar to me and a fatigue the likes of which I had never felt before. I wanted to drop to the ground right there and just sleep on the dewy grass.

"See you all again next month," said Mayu with a nod, then she turned on her heel and walked out of the circle and disappeared into the trees.

Everyone else seemed to follow her example as they started walking away as well.

Amaeka and I started walking towards the edge of the forest, even the leg that I wasn't using felt like it was made of led, even with my crutches.

Amaeka looked at me. "Tired, huh?"

"Exhausted," I said and chuckled.

We made our way to the car and drove home.

We went inside and I gave a dry "hey" to Bluebell, Onyx and Oliver who were sitting in the living room before making my way up the stairs and dropping down on the bed. I didn't even have the energy to pull the blanket over me before my eyes fell shut so I just lay on top of it.

The last thing I heard was my bedroom door opening, footsteps coming up to my bed and then I felt a different blanket being pulled over me. I opened my eyes with great difficulty, and I saw Bluebell closing my curtains to block out the rising sun.

I couldn't help but chuckle a bit. What a journey it had been. From being hit by a car, to being cursed by a vampire, then stalking her, somehow befriending her, finding out she and her family were responsible for the murders in my once quiet, boring town ... Finding out they were *actually* vampires, almost getting murdered several times, getting involved in a vampire feud that caused deaths, finding out and about shapeshifters and werewolves, getting *bitten* by a werewolf ... And now here I was, exhausted from my first night as a wolf, going to sleep in a bed in a house that was owned by a vampire and a werewolf, which apparently was against vampire rules ...

Bluebell, who had almost killed me, now making sure I was comfortable to sleep ... I was living with vampires, a werewolf and a shapeshifter ... No longer cursed – but one of them. One of the creatures humans were in the dark about.

One out of the two vampires that set out to kill me was dead. There was no direct threat anymore. The very creatures who were once quite literally my worst nightmare, were now my friends, my second family who took me in when they didn't have to. And it was wonderful.

Sleepily locking eyes with a smiling Bluebell across the room, holding on to the happy, safe, satisfied feeling I had, I drifted off into a deep sleep, the best one I had that year.

Content warning

This book contains content relating to:

Death and murder:
Death, dying, murder, death threats, near death experiences, decapitation, dead bodies, skeletons, non-human animal remains, human remains, child death, child murder, non-human animal death, non-human animal murder, loss of a loved one, death of a sibling, exposing of bodies, burning bodies.

Physical injury, abuse and gore:
Mention of stabbing and piercing and cutting and biting, mention of electrocution and drowning and getting stabbed and getting shot, mention of implied domestic abuse, mention of rape, self-injurious behaviour and acts of self-harm, scars, (described) blood, gore, graphic injuries, torture, getting shot, car accident (drunk driving), hospitalization, physical assault, attacking/ambushing, (escalating/extreme) violence/fighting, graphic death, mutilation, child abuse, non-consensual touch of a dead child, intentional transmission of infection.

Mental injury and abuse:
Toxic/abusive family relationships, manipulation, mental/emotional/verbal abuse, loss of self-control (resulting in murder), mental illness, anxiety, (onset of) depression, declining mental health, addictive feelings, nightmares, co-dependency, mention of addiction, mentions of suicide, suicidal thoughts, suicidal ideation, suicidal behavior, trauma, traumatized person, selective mutism.

Criminal abuse:
Kidnapping, abduction, people missing, stalking, drugging someone against their will (use of chloroform).

Other:
Speciesism, nudity.

Please consider that there may be topics that I have missed and
please remember to practice self-care always.

De auteur

James Aurelien was born in Amsterdam in 1998.
He has a background in animal care and is involved
in animal rights activism. His favourite activities are
writing stories and lyrics, singing and trying out
new vegan foods.
Although James Aurelien has been writing stories
and fantasy fiction for years, this is his first
published work.

De uitgeverij

Wie ophoudt
beter te worden
is opgehouden
goed te zijn!

Op basis van dit motto zoekt uitgeverij novum steeds nieuwe manuscripten! Ondertussen zijn wij in Nederland, Duitsland, Oostenrijk en Zwitserland dé specialist voor nieuwe auteurs.

Elk manuscript dat wij ontvangen wordt gratis door onze redactie beoordeeld.

Meer informatie over onze uitgeverij en over onze boeken kunt u op online vinden onder:

www.novumpublishing.nl